FLEET ACADEMY
Volume One

FAMILY

T.M. Thomas

ISBN: 0615709540
ISBN-13: 978-0615709543

Chapter 1

Anna Cosgrove-Wroclaw wished she'd changed from her jogging clothes as the cool air of the conference room swirled. The summons to the main office had just been so surprising she'd reacted and run straight from the gym. Not even seeming to notice the cold air, her fraternal twin Steve just stared at the art on the walls. It was a famous laser-etched hologrammatic painting of the Battle of Io, from the perspective of the losing side. The ships hung a few inches off the wall, one spewing bright sparks that rotated as the ship took more fire. Steve had on a cadet's regulation uniform, proper and polished. Even though he was off for the day. Typical. Anna thought about saying something to him, but the serious-looking guard made her reconsider teasing her brother.

"Are you sure I don't have time to change?" Anna asked. Ensign Mayberry shook his head, but didn't say anything. Anna didn't like the way his blue eyes kept watching her. Normally, he was a charming lecher. He teased her a lot. Now he looked almost afraid. Not of her. Maybe for her? She couldn't really read the expression and it bugged her. She always prided herself on that skill.

"I'm glad you're here," a woman's voice called out. Anna saw the quick tension in her brother's face. The door slid open a second later and two people entered.

Mayberry saluted. The man ignored him. The woman, who wasn't in uniform, returned it with textbook crispness.

"Good day, students," the man said. Anna didn't recognize him, but Steve nodded.

"Headmaster," he greeted. Anna had to look again to see the handsome man from the official portraits in the worn grey face. It was there, but buried. Like most of the instructors, he wore a plain shipside uniform without much in the way of rank or insignia.

"Admiral Cosgrove has requested to speak to you. This is highly unusual, but…," he let the end hang. Everything was unusual when "Iron Betty" Cosgrove was around. "Please try to limit the visit, Admiral. We have exams starting soon, if you don't mind."

The look Betty Cosgrove gave him made it clear that she didn't care what he thought. Anna knew the look. There was a chain of command in the Fleet and then there was Betty Costgrove.

"Hi Mom," Steve said. Anna stood and saluted.

"Remember your place, Sephalos," she told Steve. "Don't be such a suck up, Anna."

Anna looked at her brother and Steve rolled his eyes. She tried to hide her smile and keep the laughter down. "Enough," Betty said, sitting on the conference table to face them. She was wearing a skirt suit that looked very soft and fancy. The skirt was short and Anna could make out the five tattoos on her mother's legs, from ankle up to thigh. One for each winning campaign against the separatist forces. Anna saw how the headmaster checked out her legs, too. Betty saw too, Anna could tell, from the little smile. Steve saw it too. His look wasn't happy at all. His thick eyebrows knitted together and his mouth almost puckered in anger. Anna thought about reaching out to him, but the look passed quickly.

"May we have a moment?" Betty asked. Mayberry saluted instantly. The headmaster looked a little upset to be excluded, but followed the young officer out a second later.

"That young man certainly had eyes for you. I hope you're being careful." She started before the two men were out and long before the door sealed.

"Mother, I'm 15 and...," Anna blurted, going red.

"I know how old you are, dear. I missed my own 20 year reunion from this school to spend three days in bed giving birth to two giant-headed babies."

"I'm not dating any of the instructors, mother."

"I would, but they keep declining," Steve added. Betty turned her blue eyes onto the taller twin and Anna had to smile a little. Steve was always the red flag that distracted Mom when she was charging. And still ended up the favorite.

"I know about you and Ms. Jefferson, Sephalos. Be smart. But that's asking a lot," she sighed. "I'm here to tell you something important, and I need you both to be serious."

"Yes, ma'am," they answered in unison. Steve smirked a little when Betty started to look angry, thinking they were playing twin games on her, but she let it go fast.

"You will hear a lot of news over the next few days. And probably a lot more rumor. Ignore it all."

"News of what?" Steve asked.

"Does it matter, Sephalos? Why do you always question me?"

"Because I don't understand what I'm supposed to ignore." He said it slowly and calmly, meeting her bright blue eyes with his own dark eyes. The big difference between the fraternal twins, other than gender, was that Steve had their father's dark eyes and Anna looked a lot more like Iron Betty. Anna wasn't sure if it worked for or against her at the Academy, but she knew people noticed.

Betty sighed. "You're right, I was not very clear. I'm not always good at talking to kids, especially when I have a lot on my mind."

Steve nodded. Anna did too, but she didn't think it was much of an apology or explanation.

"Fleet Security has a confirmed location for Gannar Trilouis. A fugitive recovery team has been dispatched to return him for trial."

Steve made a little beep noise. Anna didn't know what sort of noise she made, but her mother was looking at her sternly. "Watch your mouth, child."

"I'm sorry. Where is he?"

"That doesn't matter. What does matter is that he'll be in custody within the week."

"Can we see him?" Steve snorted again as she asked.

"Listen, both of you. You are to focus on getting stellar grades and redeeming your family name by building strong careers. Whatever you hear, you are to say nothing. You are to pretend you know nothing. The fugitive unit will take their prisoner to a secret location for a military tribunal. I told you a long time ago this was going to happen eventually."

Anna felt a tear. She sniffed quick and willed herself to stop. Steve just looked at Betty with wide eyes.

"Don't be dramatic, either of you. Gannar Trilouis is a traitor. He deserves everything that is coming to him and I hope it comes to him soon. Robert Gannar would be rolling in his grave if he knew what the boy I'd named for him had become."

"He's still your son," Steve said, slowly. Anna wondered if he saw Betty talking about him this way in his mind. She'd heard it enough herself after she'd been caught corresponding with Gannar a couple years ago.

"He stopped being my son when he turned his back on everything that was important to me," Betty said. Steve nodded. Anna felt the tears burn on the corners of her eyes again. Not because of Gannar. Because what was important to Betty was the Fleet and the people that ran it. Not two fifteen year olds. She wondered if the message her mother was sending out ever crossed the Admiral's mind. Or if she cared if it did.

"We won't say anything," Anna said.

"We appreciate you letting us know," Steve said.

"Very good, children. Study hard and I'll arrange for you to visit your father's spacedock this spring." She hugged each one, with strong arms that felt like ropes wrapped around iron bars. She was in amazing shape. She was taller than both of them, too.

"Are you still here?" she barked as she went out the door and they heard the headmaster sputter. Then the two of them walked away, boots clanking on the metal catwalks of the academy. Mayberry leaned in and winked at Anna, then the door slid shut again.

"That guy is creepy."

"He's only a couple years older than us, Steve," Anna said, not sure why she was defending him. He was creepy when he watched her jogging or always managed to meet her outside of her classrooms. He could be sweet, too, but the way he watched her sometimes made her a little wary.

"A couple years means a lot right now," Steve said. The way he said it made Anna think he was quoting someone.

"So what about Jeecey?"

"What about him, Anna?"

"We might never see him again."

Steve smiled. "If they catch him, Anna. They will someday, but he's smart."

"It's not funny."

"It sort of is, Anna. He's been out there for almost two years, a step ahead all the time. Everything he does reflects back on us."

"And that's a good thing?" she said, slapping her hands down on the table.

"Of course. We're here. We're model students. We have two parents who are greatly respected. Every time he shows how smart he is, they know we're going to be just as smart, but working for them."

"They? Them?"

"Mom's friends, Anna. The people that run the Fleet. And the government."

She shook her head. "So it comes down to getting a good appointment on a ship? Or at Command?"

"We're academy students, Anna. Everything is about that."

"He's your brother!"

"He's also someone that stole an academy shuttle and violated the neutral zone. He may have given classified materials to the enemy."

"He's still our brother," Anna said. She hated the way her voice sounded. Iron Betty never sounded like a sad little girl. Even when she'd been a sad little girl, Anna was sure.

"Half-brother, Anna. Raised by his father for a good part of his life. Just because our mother is his mother doesn't mean we're connected to him."

"Unless it helps your career?"

Steve laughed as he stood up. "I guess so, Sis. It's almost study hour, so I best get back to the dorms. I've got to proctor the freshman Nav review session. You better go finish your run so loverboy can finish getting all worked up."

Anna stuck out her tongue, but laughed. The idea of hitting the track for another twenty minutes sounded good for getting her mind in order. Even if she'd first run the track with Jeecey on her visits when he'd been a student. Then she looked at the numbers flashing on the wall clock. "No time for that. I've missed half of my Nav lab. But don't be too rough on the new kids," she smiled, knowing that nothing she could say would affect him. She stepped back out into the warmer air of the hallway as Steve laughed away behind her, doing his movie-quality villain laugh.

Chapter 2

Anna set her Navigation books down slowly, trying to stay quiet. Professor Anserton didn't look up, from where he was doing whatever he did on the days he set the class onto worksheets.

"Hi, Anna," Melina Abbot said. Not softly. Everyone turned. Including the professor.

"Try to be on time next time, Cadet," the professor said in the brief moment he looked up from the backlit tablet he was working on.

Anna felt the flush on her face mix with a shock of relief. She gave Melina a little smile and nod. Not a friendly greeting, but enough that she couldn't be blamed for being rude. She'd tried rude, then aggressive, first year and set a record for number of trips to the Dean of Student's office. She slid onto a stool at the lab bench, giving brief nods to the two faces across from her. All other teams had four people, which was the standard number of command-line staff on the current ships being deployed. When Marsh washed out first semester, Professor Anserton shuffled the teams to put the top three students in one group. Anna looked at the other two and sighed, without meaning to. Usually Anna didn't like having Steve breathing over her shoulder, but she would have welcomed him.

Gates smiled, with his slightly crooked teeth gleaming against his ebony skin. He massed twice as much as her and scared her with the way he relied too much on intuition in plotting courses. His size and brilliance were bound to take him far in the Fleet. "Nice you could make it," he said, sliding the worksheet over to her. Handwritten and copied on an old printer for security reasons. No one could hack the professor's brain and get the pop quizzes. Anserton often noted, with a look at Anna, it had became procedure after Gannar's two year stint at the academy.

Goerlitz looked up from her tablet long enough to glare, then went back to her calculations. Normally someone with that sort of work ethic would have made Anna happy, but Goerlitz combined it with an open contempt. She was dwarfed by Gates, but somehow exuded a lot more presence into the area. Mostly tension.

"What part should I do?" Anna asked, looking over the list of problems.

"I'm doing 1 and 2. She's doing 3," Gates smiled back. His fingers kept tapping coordinate calculations as he looked up.

"I'll do four and start 5," Anna said.

"Just do 4 right," Emma Goerlitz said quietly. She was the shortest woman in their class, with muscular shoulders and a kid's round face. That mix of size and youth hadn't served her well among the others, but she was bright.

Anna almost responded, but decided it wasn't worth it. Steve was always reminding her that everything could be a test, including dealing with difficult people. Maybe one of the academy cameras was on her right now, with someone taking notes about how she dealt with the hostility. Instead she tapped the tablet to life. The screen lit with the usual Fleet logo and starfield background. Then it beeped, a warbling sound that made everyone look.

"Problem, Cadet?" the professor asked. He still had one hand and one eye on his own tablet.

"I don't know, sir." Anna tapped the screen a couple of times, but it just stayed blank.

"Take it to tech."

"But sir," Anna started, at the same time Goerlitz said the same thing. The two of them looked at each other, just daring the other to continue. Melina gave a little giggle somewhere, earning a glare from the pair of them and the professor.

"It will be a good exercise for your partners to work shorthanded. And you're useless without the tablet, unless you can do multi-variable navigational calculations in your amazing brain?"

"I'll be back right away," she promised her partners. Gates gave her his big smile, absently checking items on his page as he did it. Emma just nodded, already lost in the intricacies of the problem. Anna looked back at Melina, who gave her a little wave that might have been friendly, if you didn't know her, on her way out.

The hallway was warm, as always, and her feet echoed as she walked down the metal walkway. "Need something?" Mayberry asked, falling into step next to her.

Anna took a deep breath, holding back the little squeak of surprise so it sounded more like a hiccup or just some weird noise. She felt the flush rising in her face. "Can I help you?"

"I'm supposed to ask you, Cadet," Mayberry said, tapping the patch on his shoulder. Fleet Security had a distinctive circular insignia, black on the tan shoulder of the uniform.

She held up the black screen. "My unit is acting up. Professor Anserton sent me to tech to get it checked."

"Navigation, huh? My least favorite."

"My brother said the same. He...nevermind."

"Sephalos? Steve, I mean?"

"No, my older brother. Half-brother, really. He hated Nav and also was in Fleet Security. After he left the Academy, I mean."

"I didn't know you...oh, wait. I hadn't put those pieces together to connect you to him."

"My brother? Jeecey?"

"Gannar Charles Trilouis, you mean? He was a year ahead of me."

Anna looked at the face as they walked. He was younger than she'd thought. Gannar had been the youngest cadet ever, but the year he should have graduated was only a couple of years ago. Mayberry had a lean face, with faint pale stubble on his cheeks and chin. There were a few freckles on his little nose, blending well with the green eyes and neatly buzzed red-blond hair.

"What you looking at?" he smiled.

Anna felt the heat in her face and a tremble in her stomach. Embarrassment, mainly. "Sorry. You're younger than I had guessed. I just didn't think you were here when he was."

"Oh, yes. I saw pretty much the whole thing. One of the epic flameouts in academy history. Sorry," he added as he watched her face. "I didn't mean to offend you. It's just...it was a big thing when I was here."

"Did you know her?" Anna asked, as she reached the door to the tech unit. The hallway smelled of oil and was warmer than the surrounding area. She stopped and turned, looking up four or five inches into his thin face.

"Just from seeing her around," he said. He looked down when he said it. Not at her, but the ground. "Very pretty girl," he said after a moment, looking down into Anna's eyes. "Sort of like you."

"Thanks," she said, just as the door behind her slid open. Steve stepped out, his tablet clutched to his side.

"What's going on?" he asked. His eyes went straight to the ensign. Steve was almost as tall and much bulkier. Anna knew he liked how he could be intimidating just by standing and glaring.

"Just talking. My tablet fuzzed out."

"Mine too," Steve said. "Tech couldn't fix it and gave me a temp replacement."

"I better get mine and get back to class," she said. "Goerlitz is going to freak out if she ends up doing more than her share of the work."

"Yes, you should," her brother added. "Ensign," he said, then walked down the hallway with his usual fast step. The two of them watched until her turned the corner, the silence lengthening.

"He's very protective," Mayberry smiled.

"I better get moving though. He was right about that," Anna said, slipping through the door and leaving the ensign standing in the hall.

"Took you long enough," Mr. Entwhistle said, from the giant desk in the front of the room. Behind him, separated from the room by very clean glass, a dozen men and women worked hard at benches like in the classrooms. Entwhistle was a stooped little man with a spotted bald head, but his voice was surprisingly strong. His straggly hair, which was mainly a fringe around the tops of his ears, stretched into a long braid that ran down his back.

"I'm sorry, sir. I ran into...," she started.

"I don't really care, Cadet. No offense. When you and your brother have the same problem, my curiosity is piqued. I want to take a look."

"Here it is," she said, stepping forward to hand it over. Entwhistle reached out to grab it and Anna saw the familiar tattoo on the inside of his wrist. The Battle of Io logo, just like the one her mother wore. Entwhistle had been a senior engineer aboard her flagship. She'd heard his name a thousand times before coming here.

He smiled when he saw her looking at the smudgy mark on his wrist. "It looked a lot better when I was younger and still had some muscle tone."

"My mother told me you were on the crew. She likes to let me know who at the academy is a veteran."

"Officially, I should say everyone is a veteran here. We're all Fleet officers or retirees. But knowing your mother, I can guess what she means. The ones that saw fire or lived under her command. Which was sort of like being under fire."

"I think so," she said.

"Not bad advice if you want to be an officer, Cadet. Anyone can learn from a book, but command takes some real experience."

"What would you tell me, Sir?"

"As a retired Lt. Commander, I'd tell you," he said, pausing to tap the tablet to life, "get back to class or you'll never get a ship posting." He tapped a few times and it stayed dead. He reached into the desk and pulled out a plain black plastic unit.

"Yes sir," she smiled back, taking the replacement unit he was holding out.

"I'll leave a message for you to come pick this up when I've got it back online again. Now seriously, get back to class."

Anna saluted, which wasn't entirely necessary to the retiree, but he snapped it back with cool efficiency.

Mayberry wasn't in the hall when she left, which wasn't what she expected. She thought the tall, thin man would be waiting with a smile. A little shiver ran down her spine as her feet echoed through the metal hallways. It was warm and smelled of freshly scrubbed air, but it felt extra empty and a little lonely. She didn't know why she felt the sad feeling tugging at her stomach, but she knew it didn't really put her in the mood for more math. Too bad class rank and all the associated privileges depended on putting up with Gates' guesses and Goerlitz's anger the rest of the session.

"About time," Melina said in a little voice as she slipped back into the room. Anna ignored her. They'd been friends for about an hour after first arriving, until Melina had found some girls more likely to follow her. Melina had decided after the first few minutes that her attitude was going to be her calling card. Her grades had made that easier, Anna had heard from Steve, who knew her fairly well. Not bad enough to fail out, but there was no way she'd ever make the Honors track that would put her in command of a ship. Melina's cohort giggled a little, earning a look from where the professor was tapping quickly on his tablet.

"Where are we?" Anna asked, sliding into her seat.

"We're done," Gates said, handing over his tablet. "Just waiting for you."

He smiled when he said it. He had high grades and wasn't as laid back as he acted, she knew. No one made it here with that attitude. "Thanks for waiting," she said, as if three or four screaming matches hadn't resulted in Anna always checking his work before it was handed in. Gates had told her he wanted to be a commander, too, so he wasn't going to raise any issues in public.

"Off by a third here," Anna said to herself, tapping away, "and a fraction here, but they cancel. It checks. Emma?"

"I looked twice. Looked good to me."

"Send it," Anna said. Emma paused, and Anna wondered if it had sounded too much like an order. No one wanted to be submissive when there were only three or four command postings for each class. Then the smaller girl clicked a few buttons on her pad and submitted the answers.

Professor Anserton grimaced as the arrival interrupted whatever he was working on at his desk. "I'll grade it later. You can go now."

"Do we have any assignments?" Gates asked, picking up his tablet and a big stack of books. Emma groaned and Anna couldn't help but smile. Gates was that kid in every class. The way he asked with a big smile, like he enjoyed the work, made it hard for her to complain. Much.

The professor sighed in frustration, sounding sort of like Emma. He held a finger on his tablet as he looked up, not wanting to stop his work. "This goes for everyone. Review your problems overnight. I'll let you revise for 1/3 credit tomorrow if you feel you need to fix anything. Because you're all grade-obsessed and to remind you that, even if your math puts a cruiser into a sun, you're still students and the goal is to learn."

Anna saluted, but the professor just waved her off. "Freeloader," Melina said as the threesome left the room, but Anna didn't bother to acknowledge her. Emma did, Anna noted. Just a little smile and, but she saw it. And how Melina shut out the uncool girl with a glare that made it clear they weren't on the same side.

"Sorry about today," Anna said as soon as they were in the hall. "I don't know what went wrong with my tablet. It was weird..."

"Save it," Goerlitz said, adjusting her uniform skirt and blouse. Very few women chose anything other than the unisex jumpsuits. Betty Cosgrove wore a lot of skirts, though, so there were always a few. It looked good on her, Anna thought, but she knew better than to say it. Emma heard everything as an insult.

"I appreciate you both not making a deal out of it," Anna said.

"And what? Complain about Admiral Cosgrove's little girl? We want jobs when we graduate."

Anna squared her shoulders and looked at the other girl. "I pull my weight, Emma. You know that."

"That's not what happened today."

"Once in three years? And you're pulling this?"

"Let's just make sure it doesn't happen again," Gates said. Anna turned to look at him, hands on hips, then saw the look in his eyes. He was just trying to get them to stop. Anna almost laughed.

"No problem. Apologies to you both," Anna said, mainly at Gates.

"That's not going to do it."

"What is your problem, Goerlitz?"

"I heard the news, Anna."

"What news?"

"Your mother was here. You're being given a command next month."

Anna snorted. It was supposed to be a laugh. "My mom was here, but there's no command."

"Really? Then why are four brand-new ships hovering by Bay 3?"

Anna paused, surprised. "I don't know anything about that."

"Me either," Gates said with a cautious slowness. "How do you, Emma?"

She flushed, but recovered quickly. "I went out with one of the Petty Officers, okay? He works in the bays. He says there are four ships just waiting, always at battlestations."

"That doesn't have anything to do with me."

"Does it?"

"No!" Anna said. "Why would it?"

Emma paused a moment. "I don't know. I heard your mother was here, and then there's ship traffic near the school. Something is going on."

"No question. But I'm just a student like you."

Emma nodded, but didn't say anything more as she stalked away. Gates gave one of his anxious little smiles and walked off in the other direction.

Chapter 3

"Are you certain you want to submit this as your answer?"

Steve lowered his replacement tablet to look into the round face of his biology lab partner. "Did I send it to you?"

Josette Jefferson leaned back in her chair, bending backwards until her back cracked and popped three times. Steve's eyes were glued to her curves as she moved. Then she leaned back forward, her green eyes meeting up with Steve's own dark eyes. "Yes, you did. And you have too many ATP molecules in the terraforming model."

Steve pulled the tablet back up and ran through his notes. "It's an enriched mix, from problem 2. Basic photosynthetic math for such genetically modified bacteria."

"The enrichment you used isn't stable enough to produce that much ATP."

"Fine, then. Use standard numbers at two and take out the extra molecule. Set science back twenty years." He said it with earnest seriousness. She laughed. He gave a little sad noise like a whining puppy. She laughed again.

"Done," she said, as soon as his drone finished. She hit a few more keys on the flat panel. "It's off to Dr. Wilson. What's next?"

Steve looked around the library. It was empty. No one was pulling the heavy historical books off the shelves or studying at any of the metal tables bolted around the edges of the room. "That was the last lab. We have an hour or so. Perhaps you can put literature back twenty years while we wait."

Josette laughed. "You really are funny."

"Hardly."

"You still have those photos on your tablet?"

"Not mine. This is a temp replacement."

Her face flushed. "So...tech has them?"

"Relax. They are on my personal server."

She smiled, switching chairs from across the table to take the one next to him. She had her shoes off and curled up on the chair, leaning close. "Sorry, Seph," she said. "I know, you hate that nickname."

"No, I hate being called 'Sephalos.'"

"It's a cool name," she said, putting a hand on his knee. "Everyone knows who Captain Sephalos was."

"No," he said, leaning in to stroke the side of her face. With her hair so newly short, it felt odd to not have the familiar weight of her hair on his hand. "Everyone here does. No one outside the Fleet knows of some Gunnery officer that my mother favored."

"A gunnery officer who selflessly died laying cover fire to protect the Fleet's regroup," she said, straddling his lap. She was short but curvy, from the round face down to the gentle swell of her muscular legs. She hated the way it made her look younger than her classmates, she'd said repeatedly. Steve had laughed each time and told her she was a freshman and they were all just babies anyway, even if she was advanced enough to merit his tutoring. "You're going to be a commander like that someday. Doing great things."

Her lips were sweet. A moment later it was her sweet tongue Steve tasted as she pressed against him. His hands were on her hips, holding her closer to him.

"When are you taking me to Flight Deck?" she breathed into his ear.

Steve felt the blood rush fading. "Jo, I'm...I'm not ready for that."

She went red as he looked embarrassed. "I'm sorry, Steve. I just get caught up," she said, and leaned in for another kiss.

"This is not appropriate," a voice barked. Josette jumped up, kicking Steve in the knee. Steve gritted his teeth, grabbing the knee as he hopped up, turned and saluted.

Captain Morris looked angry. Even worse, he looked mussed. Captain Morris was a fashion plate. Now his Fleet Security jacket was open and his academy staff badge crooked.

"I'm sorry, Sir," Steve started.

"I was sent to find you, Cadet, and I'll ignore all of this, once.

Understood?"

"Yes sir."

"As for you, Cadet...you'd better think twice before trying to land a husband in that family."

Josette went red and it showed, even with her African coloring. Steve wasn't sure if she was embarrassed or angry. "Sir, I..."

"Let it go, Cadet Jefferson. Get back to your studies. You, though, are coming with me."

"How can I help you, sir?" Steve saluted. Just like with his mother, Morris paused, not sure if it was serious or not.

"You're going to answer some questions, Cadet, about some odd things on your tablet."

Josette went red again. This time he knew she was angry. She didn't believe him about the pictures they'd taken. Steve knew that wasn't it, though, because his mother wasn't here herself. There would have been a fleet of warships and Judge Advocates if that had been the case. And probably a fraternization trial, just to prove she was right about him.

"Of course, sir," he smiled, giving Morris the same look back that he was giving out. The captain's look hardened and he pointed, so Steve started walking.

Chapter 4

"You seem very relaxed," Captain Morris said, easing into a chair.

Steve smiled across the table at him. It was an old conference table, from one of the workrooms. Staff always scavenged the high quality leftovers from the student section. Someone had tried to buff the shine back into it, but a decade of student activity was permanently embedded in the surface. "I've seen this show before," Steve said, tilting his head at the mirror on the wall.

"We don't have a lot of places to talk that are secure, so we're using one of these rooms, ok?"

"Not at all, Captain. That's a complete lie. I could have talked to you anywhere, but you picked this room. A room equipped with subtle heart rate sensors, several cameras and, if this is according to regulation, two observers behind the screen."

"It's not regulation. We're just talking, Sephalos."

"Then I'll be leaving," Steve said, pushing the sturdy little chair back so it squeaked on the floor. The chair and tile weren't any newer than the table.

"I can't let you do that."

"I know, Captain. So why don't you just admit I'm here as a suspect in yet another campus prank and we'll discuss where and how I wasn't involved?"

"I'm not Lieutenant Hines, Cadet. I don't care who short-sheeted whom. You kids can do whatever you want to each other."

Steve leaned forward, resting his chin on one hand, stroking where there wasn't yet a beard. "You say that, but you've been stationed here almost three months. So, much like your first story, something isn't matching up."

Morris waved at the mirror. Footsteps echoed in the hallway and a moment later a junior officer rushed in. She was carrying a flat black tablet, which she handed to Morris. She left without even looking at Steve. He mainly noted that because her face wasn't one he'd seen around before. As cramped as the academy was, there usually weren't any strangers during a term, when traffic was highly controlled.

"Is this your tablet?"

Steve took the rectangle of plastic and tapped the screen. As it came to lift, he tapped out a quick beat on the side of the case. A menu opened on the screen. "Appears to be."

"That's an illegal modification, by the way. Students are not permitted to tamper with the learning units."

Steve smiled back at him, ignoring the serious look. "Students are told that in the hopes of separating out the senseless order followers, the unthinking rebels and those smart enough to realize it's completely underperforming and to upgrade it."

"This one of your programs?" Morris said, keying one of the stars on the background display. A little purple box snapped into being, full of characters and symbols.

"Nothing I've seen."

"Think again before you answer me."

"Honest. I mod for speed and memory. I wouldn't ever install third party programs on a school machine." He pushed his chair back closer to the table, looking at the machine closely.

"Funny thing, that," Morris said. His long fingers danced over the screen, faster than Steve would have expected. The purple box went blue, then back to purple and then faded away. "According to every diagnostic they can run here, it's not only something you installed, but it's something that the school gave you permission to install."

"That's not true."

"This is Fleet Academy Alpha, Cadet. They have scientists here that do things most people would think is magic. Rethink that."

Steve leaned back. His hands slid a little on the table. Butterflies were dancing around his stomach now. Usually giving attitude to the officers was all part of the game. Prove you're tougher than them and you get a job better than them. This didn't feel like a game anymore. "Seriously."

Morris glared for a moment. "I know," he said, his face softening. "You're smart, but this is not a one man job. Someone hacked your unit and made the Security system think it was all ok."

"I didn't do anything like that."

"I'm believing you now, Cadet. I'd have been shocked if you knew, but I have to be cautious."

"Thank you, Sir. My future career is very important to me. I'd never do anything to jeopardize it."

"Even if family was involved?"

"Anna? She's not...," Steve started, but Morris raised one of those long fingers.

"No, not her. Your brother."

"Gannar Trilouis and I have nothing to do with each other, Captain."

"And you're certain?"

"More than anything."

"Very good, Cadet. Get back to your classes. Keep using the replacement tablet for now. We'll be in touch if we know more, but I trust you know not to say anything."

"Of course, Captain. Thank you."

"Keep your hands off the underclassman, too, Mr. Cosgrove. It's poor taste for a proctor to be seen having a bias."

Steve fled, barely waiting for the door to slide open before he was into the metal walkways and heading back toward the student side of the academic station. He could feel Captain Morris watching him from the door, but he kept going until he reached the lift.

Chapter 5

Anna took a long breath and waited, balancing the rubber ball on her hand. Melina moved first. She rolled, then somersaulted, landing on her feet next to another bright orange ball. By the time she had it in her hand, Anna had her own arm in motion.

The ball caught Melina in the face. "Ow!" she howled, falling over, just as the whistles blew from the teaching staff.

"Game! Blue wins," Ms. Ashland said, giving Anna a thumbs up. "Red, ten laps."

"Ms. Ashland, maybe Melina should," Anna started, but Ashland stopped her.

"Are you a winner or a loser, Cadet?"

"My team won."

"So you didn't win?" the teacher asked. She was younger than most of the professors, only a few years older than the cadets. All of boys loved her little blonde cut and athletic build. Most of the girls hated her attitude.

"I won."

"Then why do you care about the losers?"

Anna sighed. The instructor's sour mouth puckered a little more.

"Ten laps, Cadet. Maybe you'll learn to respect winning."

Anna nodded and started the run around the gym. With the dividers in place, it wasn't very far. The point wasn't that it was strenuous. They just were trying to drive more wedges, she knew.

"You ok?" Anna asked Melina, who was holding her tee-shirt to her nose. "I didn't mean to get you there."

"A week before Spring Formal you didn't try to break my nose?"

"I didn't. I don't care about that."

Melina's green eyes were like jade rocks. "I know you didn't. You'd have to be going first to care and no one would ask you."

"Run, ladies!" Ashland yelled, from where she was talking to the other teachers.

Anna started moving. She was surprised when Melina caught up and stayed beside her a second later. The tee shirt was gone entirely, but the bleeding had stopped. There was a stripe of blood under her nose, but Anna noticed it didn't keep the boys from watching Melina run by.

"Why aren't you going to the dance, Anna?" Anna was surprised by the question. It seemed a legit inquiry.

"You said it yourself. No one would ask."

"Maybe. But it's because you don't care. I've never met a girl that didn't care."

"Maybe I'm just weird."

Melina snorted.

"Why are you talking to me now, anyway? Some sort of masochist that liked having your nose moved around?"

Melina just snorted again. They rounded the corner near the teachers and were quiet for a moment.

"I've seen you hanging out with some guys before. You aren't a total freak. I think you know something. The dance is another test, isn't it?"

"What do you mean?"

"The cadets who go are docked points or something, for not being serious enough?"

"I doubt it." Anna laughed, which drew a look from the teachers.

Melina was quiet a moment as they rounded another corner. "No, really."

"As excited as my mom gets about the formals, Melina, I can safely say it's not a test. She loves parties and thinks everyone should."

"I can't picture your mom at a dance."

"She's just my mom, Melina. She's like anyone else," Anna said, but she knew that wasn't really true. Melina's little smirk made her know she wasn't really believed, either.

"You're lucky to have family in the Fleet. It's hard for an outsider," Melina said.

"Really? I thought they had open admission."

Melina's look was withering. Anna flushed just from the way her classmate looked at her, like she was a silly child. "Four slots out of eighty."

"That's all? Wow."

"And here I am, already knowing I'm not going to graduate to a ship and you could skip the rest of the year and still pass."

"Melina, that's not true," Anna said.

"Please. You're Cosgrove's kid. You could do no wrong."

Anna frowned. "You don't know how wrong that is."

"Please," Melina repeated, with the full wither. Her green eyes were cold.

They reached the corner at the same time and slowed, walking along the gym wall to cool down. "You know I have a brother?"

"Steve? He's cute. A little nerdy," Melina said.

Anna shrugged like she had a chill. "Please don't say that about him. But not him. Our older brother. Half-brother."

"He go here? He must. Or did he graduate?"

"Neither. Burned out so they made him a part-time Security officer to keep him busy. Then he failed out and ran away. Stole a shuttle to do it."

Melina's eyes grew big. "I thought that was just a story the seniors told. It's real?"

"It's real. So don't think that who I am gets me a free pass. If anything, they are watching and testing me more closely."

"Is that why you're such a bitch?"

"Excuse me? Me? You haven't said two pleasant words in three years."

"Yes, you. Your stuck up attitude and tight little outfits, hanging out all over like you don't notice. It's not enough that you have the family and all the great grades. But you pretend you don't see the way all the guys follow you."

"I don't notice. And I'm not stuck up. You're stuck up!"

"Me? I have more friends than anyone here."

"Sure, but you hate anyone not in your group."

"Because they were mean to me first!"

The two of them stared at each other. "Maybe I was wrong about you," Anna said. "You suck, but in a different way than I thought."

"Yeah. Maybe I should have gotten to know you first. So I'd know what a total bitch you are in person." She sort of laughed as she said it, though.

"I'm sorry about your face. I hope it doesn't mess things up at the spring formal."

"It's ok. It's not going to leave a mark. Besides, I haven't had a boyfriend since Ingmar shipped out last year. We're supposed to be still together, but he can't make it back."

"We could go?"

Melina's eyes grew wide. "I'm not...!"

"Me either!" Anna laughed. "I just meant we could hang out together or something if we aren't going with anyone. I could be less weird, if you'd like. I'm trying to reach out and be a better person."

"Could be," Melina said, picking up the discarded tee shirt from the benches. "If I don't get a better offer." She strutted out and Anna was left trying to figure out if she was serious or not.

"Who's that?" Steve asked, a moment later.

"Melina. She's in most of my classes."

Steve walked in, stopping next to his sister. "I should have picked that track. She's hot."

"You have a girlfriend."

"Merely an observation."

"One you wouldn't say is Jo was here."

Steve shrugged. "I just wanted to stop on my way to class. They talked to you about your tablet yet?"

Anna shook her head. "No. Why? You get yours back?"

"No. There's something weird going on. Security pulled me down to talk because it had been hacked."

"Everyone hacks the tablet."

"Everyone smart, anyway. But this was something different. I think they'll be watching us now."

"We don't have anything to hide. Other than you approaching me in secret during girls' gym."

Steve startled, then laughed. "For a chance to see Melina? Worth a covert mission."

"Jerk," she laughed, as the bell rang. "I'm going to be late."

"As usual," her twin said, strolling off to class like it wasn't his problem.

Chapter 6

Serg lifted the apples off the cart carefully, while the bigger boys were causing a scene at the front of the market. All it had taken was a couple coins thrown on the ground. Or metal disks that looked a lot like coins. He'd been too busy watching the men who'd thrown the coins to care about the prize. He heard a shopkeeper yell, maybe even the little woman that sold fruit, but his feet were already moving. He was already back at the foundation of the great brick tower when the police sirens howled to announce the cops arriving. A few little rocks pulled easily out of place, making a door big enough for him to barely fit through. He closed with a grunt and all the might of his little body. He heard yells and screams as the police raced into the market, stun rods and shock pistols ready.

"What did they get?" his big brother asked, sitting up on the little bed they took turns sharing.

"Diversion was next to the junk dealer, so something electronic," Serg said. He was barely four feet tall at eight years old, but his voice sounded much older. High, but measured and thoughtful. He was wearing old clothes that were cut down or tied off to fit on his little body and his mop of blond hair hadn't been cut in ages. He did keep it washed to keep the bugs and smells away. He'd seen the boys that didn't get eaten from the inside out.

"That doesn't narrow it down much."

Serg shrugged. "I didn't dare get close enough to check after way they chased me last time."

"You shouldn't have stolen their navigation circuitry, then."

"You told me too."

His houseguest laughed. "True enough. Listening to me is going to get you in a lot of trouble."

Serg bit into an apple, letting his eyes answer. Trouble wasn't something new. "So how long before you get it running?"

"Get what running, Sergei?"

"How should I know? But you've been very precise with the things you've been having me get. And things you want me to watch what the odd old men are collecting. You've also been reading that green book a lot."

"Can you read?"

"Of course I can read. Not whatever language that thing is in, though," he finished after a moment, looking a little sad.

"I'll show you once we're in the air," his brother said, rubbing the smaller boy on the head. Serg faked he was pulling away, but he didn't. "You didn't need to risk stealing that apple, though. We have plenty of food. They might have seen you."

"They did see me. If I went from stealing every meal to not being seen, someone would worry."

"I don't think anyone here worries, Serg. This place makes my home look charming."

"Everyone worries about me. I'm too cute," he smiled.

His brother laughed. "Just another tool in your toolbox."

"Weapon in my arsenal, Dad said."

They both laughed for a moment. "Trust a soldier to make everything about war."

"You're not a soldier?" Serg asked. He ran his hands along the military jacket that his brother had draped over the back of their only chair.

"I'm a pilot, if we ever get the rest of the nav circuits I need."

Serg smiled. "There. All you needed to do was be honest, big brother. I know a guy across town that isn't cheap, but can help us."

"He able to keep this quiet?"

"I don't deal with anyone else," the little boy nodded. Gannar Trilouis couldn't help but laugh at the serious look on the little face.

Chapter 7

"This is the most happy you've looked all week," Gates said as they stepped off the lift.

Anna turned her smile to him. Today, nothing could bother her. "It's simulators, Gates."

"It's just another Navigation exercise."

Goerlitz didn't say anything as they walked. Anna saw a sour look on occasion, but she was quiet. Anna didn't know why, but it was nice.

"It's not just another exercise. It's a chance to operate the simulators."

"I don't get you at all," Gates laughed. Anna joined in, for no other reason that it was simulator day.

"Welcome," Ensign Mayberry greeted them at the door.

"What are you doing here?" Anna asked, surprised. She was instantly reminded of the flight suit she wore and how she'd been accused of wearing them too tight.

"Is that a proper question for an officer, Cadet?" Mayberry asked, although he was smiling. Gates lost his smile quickly and Goerlitz just looked at the ground.

"No, Sir. I apologize."

"To answer, however, I'm taking a turn as a practicum instructor. All staff stationed here have to fill several roles. I've been meeting with teams from your class for about a week now." The unspoken comment that it wasn't just for her was clear to Anna, but she wasn't sure anyone else heard it. She hoped not.

"Strap in," Mayberry said. The simulators were eight giant corrugated metal boxes, with wires and tubes running from one to the other and to a bigger box in the corner. "Solo units today."

"Solo?" all three students asked at the same time. Gates was surprised, with his heavy black eyebrows almost pushed together in the center of his head. Anna was excited and almost skipped to one of the boxes. Out of the corner of her eye, she saw Emma Goerlitz staring at the ground as soon as the word was out of her mouth.

Mayberry picked up a tablet that was hardwired into the teacher's console at the front of the room. "Last time out, you worked in a single unit to command an assault ship defending a freighter against pirates. New York-class, requiring a crew of how many?"

"Seventy-five," they all answered at once.

"Four pilots, a navigation team of five and six gunnery officers," Gates added.

"Very good," Mayberry said. "Your team scored one of the highest scores ever on that simulation. You work well together. So today we're going to change the rules a bit."

Goerlitz raised her hand. Mayberry nodded. "I thought the syllabus said today was the A-98 carrier."

"It is, Cadet. You're just not flying the carrier itself. Now, strap in."

Anna jumped through the door quickly, hitting the familiar green button that pulled it shut behind her. There were five chairs in the box, each with a variety of wires and cables. It was almost second nature for her to clip the leads into place on the hardwired simulator suit and fit the helmet and goggles over her head. As soon as she did, everything was pitch black. From memory, she hit the red button next to her chair.

The view sprang to life instantly. One moment it was all black. The next she looked out the screen of a small ship. P-34 Storm, she recognized.

"P-34 Storm. One man assault craft. Two burners forward, one rear. Capable of carrying three standard missles. Fuel range 2,000 kilometers," Gates said in her ear.

"I'm not rated to pilot this class of ship," Goerlitz echoed.

Anna was still looking out the screen, or at least the computer simulation of the view screen. The massive command tower of the A-98 carrier was in front of her, with a half-dozen other Storms and other craft on the deck. She hit the virtual controls and swiveled. Behind, a complex airlock and elevator was bringing more Storms to the surface for launch.

"I skipped loading and suit checks because I just want this to be about the flight," Mayberry said through the speaker in her ear. "Mission is simple. Routine patrol grid, appearing now."

Anna nodded to herself as it flashed onto the screen around her. Each team of Storms would do a series of boxes, circling around the carrier to check for potential harm.

All around, the screen lit as the engines fired on groups of fighters. Anna ran through the check herself, running her fingers across keys and buttons that appeared before her eyes. She knew they weren't really there, but they felt like they were. The flight suit was plugged in so that resistance from a key or throttle felt real.

"Alpha go," Gates said, appointing himself lead. One of the Storms to her left roared to life, lifting vertically off the deck and then powering forward into the star-dotted black.

"Beta go," Anna said, following his trajectory off the ship. Most of flight at this point was just letting inertia take hold when the magnetic dampers let the ship loose from the deck. She felt the little vertigo that came from moving off the "ground" of the ship. It gave her goosebumps and brought a smile to her face.

"Gamma go," Goerlitz said. Anna watched the third ship behind her. Emma's ship turned and started to lift, then wobbled. "Gamma to tower," she started.

"Gamma check," Mayberry said.

There was no response. The ship spun twice and crashed back onto the flight deck. The fireball consumed about four other Storms and a few smaller ships.

"You ok, Emma?" Gates asked.

"She can't hear you," Mayberry answered. "You two complete the grid."

"It's normally a four ship...," Anna began.

"Do it," Mayberry said. He sounded like a regular teacher then.

Anna felt the ship arc gently when she applied pressure to the controls. The Storm was all keypad based, without the manual stick control of most fighters. Her mother hated it, as a pilot. Her father loved it, as an engineer.

"Clear Alpha," Gates said after a few minutes. They were working in tandem, a helix pattern that circled the gridlines appearing on the virtual screens.

"Intruder Charlie," a voice called out. It startled Anna so much she jumped and her ship wobbled. Maybe she agreed with her mother on the keypad controls.

"Responding," Gates said. He peeled down, toward the grid calling for help. She followed a moment behind, watching the engines of the various other ships all turning. She kept scanning the sky around for whatever was causing the distress call, but all she saw was the familiar blue flame of the Fleet ships.

"Alert!" another computerized voice called. Anna went into evasive out of habit, rolling left. The barrel roll didn't show anything but more blue flame.

Then the explosions started.

Anna jerked the controls, smashing at the buttons, shocked at the balls of flame erupting around her. Each was a little blossom of blue and red, fading quickly. Dozens of temporary stars filled her screen as hot debris filled the spaces for a few moments, before disappearing as it cooled.

"Alpha?" she called, then raised her hand to hit the frequency button. "Storm 433 checking. Status?"

The secure Fleet channel was just static. She wheeled the Storm around, feeling sweat running down her forehead and on the small of her back. All around was just black space, with a few unblinking lights that could have been stars. Or could have been the running lights of a dozen destroyers. Or could have been missiles locked on her radio signal. She tapped the screens, but it all read as empty. Something was jamming the signals.

She dipped the Storm, setting a course back to the carrier. She spun and dove, then swung a parabolic arc. Twice she hit the button that dropped flashes and flares behind her, to throw off any missile guidance systems.

"Carrier, Storm 433. Please respond. This is Storm 433. We are under attack."

Silence.

She checked the coordinates, zipping the Storm into an arc that covered a few thousand yards in a second. The carrier filled her screen suddenly as she righted the Storm. A second ship was next to it. She recognized the A-23 carrier. Very old and too small to carry the modern attack ships, but there were a few still in use through the Fleet.

"A-98. A-23. This is Storm 433. Please respond."

She saw the flag a moment later. The A-23 had looked dark to her, and she'd thought it shadow from where it was obscured behind the newer Fleet carrier. It changed as she closed in. It didn't have the blue Fleet flag on the hull. It had a black scar, where the flag had been burnt away, taking all the miniature trackers and electronics embedded in the paint with it. The flag that replaced it was a deep red rectangle, with four white stars along the bottom.

Anna jerked the controls, but it was too late. Four Scream fighters appeared from under the A-98, cutting towards her at top speed, already firing their burner guns in blinking blue flashes. She didn't feel more than a jerk, although the screen lit up with a fiery death that made her sweat even more.

"What did we learn today?" Mayberry said in her ear. The lights were still off, but she started to remove the leads and connectors with shaky hands.

"That you cheat," a deep voice responded after a moment of quiet.

Mayberry laughed. "And why is that, Mr. Gates?"

"We didn't see that coming. Normally proximity sensors would have been ringing like crazy."

"Sure, if you're on the bridge. In a fighter, you only know what they tell you."

"And they wouldn't tell us if a friendly was approaching," Gates admitted.

"Anyone know what that was?"

Goerlitz answered first. Her voice was soft and a little breathy. Anna wondered if she had been crying. "The carrier was too new, but it looked like Titan 4."

Anna remembered the history lesson and ran it through her mind. It had been an A-42 carrier and an A-23, but the rest was accurate. The 98 had replaced the 42 only a year or so ago.

"What happened next, Cadet Gates?"

"The Separatist forces destroyed the carrier and all its ships, before advancing on Io Base."

"Where?"

"This is Navigation, not History," Anna added. "Sir. With all due respect, I mean," she corrected.

"It is Navigation, Cadet. So what happened next?"

"The carrier met up with two other separatist ships and engaged the Fleet defense force at Io."

"And?"

"All three Separatist ships were destroyed."

"How? Cadet Goerlitz?"

There was a drinking sound on the radio for a moment, then she coughed. "Fission bomb. It is still visible as a radioactive anomaly in the fifth quadrant of Io's space."

"And now we're back to Navigation. If you ever fly near Io, what do you have to do?"

"Avoid sensor flight. Use radio signals or hardwired maps," all three answered at once. It was a rote answer from the earliest days of learning shuttle controls.

The simulator door popped open. Anna was surprised, as always, how fresh the air smelled in the room outside the little box. She stood and stretched, embarrassed at how wet her butt felt from all the sweat. It hadn't even been a half hour and she felt like she'd been running miles.

Gates was stretching outside his box when she emerged, looking none the worse. She wished he didn't irritate her so much, because he did seem like a good guy. He just often acted like the Academy was a fun game he was playing and not his life. Goerlitz was already sitting next to her simulator. Her little freckled chipmunk cheeks were almost green and she held a cup of water. Next to her was a garbage bin, held close enough to make Anna sure she'd been throwing up.

They stood and waiting while Mayberry ran through a few more screens on his tablet. "Not a bad job, for the most part."

Goerlitz stared at the ground again.

"I'll like to have a talk with you," Mayberry said, looking at her until she looked up. "You other two, go clean up. Decent work. I'll write up a report for you later today."

Gates and Anna both stopped to put a hand on Emma's shoulder on the way by, but no one said much. Anna didn't know what had happened. She knew why she was so quick to walk out, and she didn't like it, but there was one thing you avoided at all costs, and that was failure. Being around it could taint your career before it ever started.

Chapter 8

"You heard anything?"

Anna closed her locker door to find her brother waiting, leaning up against the wall. The underclassman with nearby lockers hung around, waiting, but were afraid to ask him to move.

"About what?"

He gave her one of his patented looks that was all thick dark eyebrow. "Jeecey."

"You never call him that anymore. Not since you decided he should be in prison somewhere."

"Well?"

"No, I haven't heard anything. I've been busy with classes."

"You're always busy."

"You're one to talk," she said, turning down the metal walkway. Steve followed a step behind, his place filled instantly by underclassman whispering as they stared.

"What was your simulation class this week?"

"Mining for tips?"

"They wouldn't give us the same thing."

"Battle of Titan 4. Sneak attack stuff."

"Commanding a carrier?" he asked with interest that surprised her.

"Fighters."

"I hope mine is like that."

"You mean you haven't reprogrammed them all to do what you want?"

"Only the staff machines. I didn't want to tip my hand too early." He smiled, but she knew he was serious. She'd helped compile the programs containing all his override codes.

Anna stopped at the classroom door. Inside she could see Melina and her girls talking and looking at them. The rest of the class was either chatting in smaller groups or looking over their books and tablets. "I have Fleet Logistics now. I can't be late."

Steve looked into the room. "Not a lot of competition for you. You should have stayed on my track."

"We need some time apart. We drive each other nuts."

"We're related. We're supposed to. Let me know if you hear," Steve said, taking a step back and merging into the hallway traffic.

"That your brother?" Gates asked as she pulled up a chair near his table. They weren't required to stay in the same groups for every class, but she didn't have many other options.

"Of course."

"Why do you say that?" he asked, peering over the edge of his tablet.

"I thought everyone knew us."

"Academy celebrities?"

"Well, our family is pretty well known."

Gates smiled, showing those even teeth again. "I know. I was teasing, a bit. I've just never met him."

"We picked different classes this year. You know how it is with your siblings."

"Not really. I'm an only child."

"Oh. Well, sometimes we get on each other's nerves."

"Makes sense. You get on my nerves a lot."

She laughed along with him for a moment, until Captain Stetler entered. She was a stocky woman with a huge bun of red hair who always wore a formal Fleet uniform. The captain glared around the room, silencing all the chatter. "Chapter fourteen, mess accounting. Are you all prepared with your reading assignments?"

"Yes, Captain," the room answered. It was the only safe answer, Anna knew.

"What is the appropriate ratio of durable supplies to perishables on a survey mission? Ralph."

Cadet Ralph went red, but managed to sputter something out.

"You get a D for the week. Your people won't die. Cadet Abbot, same question but aboard a destroyer."

Melina didn't get red, but paused just the same as she studied her tablet. "Six to two."

"Is that the same as three to one, Cadet?"

Melina went red. "Yes, Captain."

"Wrong. You fail this week. You shouldn't even be in this class, in my opinion. The answer is three to two. You'd have a mutiny."

"I doubt it," Melina said.

"Excuse me?" the Captain responded. It was a quiet voice, very unlike the roar she used for grilling the class.

Melina's face danced through a few different shades of red. Anna almost found it amusing, other than no one should be singled out like that. Even if they brought it on themselves.

"There hasn't been a mutiny on a Fleet ship in twenty-five years."

"I would suggest you do not continue with your own mutiny, Cadet Abbot."

"No offense, Captain, but she does have a point," one of Melina's friends chimed in. Only to collapse in on herself with a look from the officer. The dark girl started to sweat as soon as the Captain fixed her with a glare.

"What is your point, Miss Abbot?"

"I was wrong in my answer. But to extrapolate that a mutiny would follow from one provisions error aboard a short-haul ship is extreme. It isn't in keeping with the realities of Fleet life we are supposed to learn."

The captain's eyes went wide and her mouth worked. Everyone in the room leaned away from her, just waiting for an explosion.

The knock on the door made everyone jump. It opened with a couple of clicks and the Headmaster was there. He looked younger and more energetic than when Anna had seen him before. "Captain, apologies, but I must borrow one of your students."

"Very well, headmaster. I was about to send certain students to you for discipline, anyway."

The headmaster cocked his head, looking down at the red-faced woman. "Is this the POW situation again?"

"No, sir," Captain Stetler said, losing some of the steel from her voice.

"The mutiny?"

"Yes, sir."

He cleared his throat and looked around the room. "Whoever brought it up, this time," he started, looking at the captain as he said it, then panning back over the students. "No, an armed rebellion over ill-fitting sheets is not likely. You are correct to that extent. However, please imagine how it would greatly impact your performance reviews and/or promotional prospects."

The room had changed. Most everyone was looking at the headmaster with a little fear for their careers. Anna saw that Captain Stetler looked afraid, too. She's been called on bad tactics by the person who oversaw her promotions, too.

"And to make it clear, you are never going to be captured as a POW by a semi-human alien race that will breed you for food, forcing you to choose between saving yourself or your captured crewmates. Correct, Captain?"

"Yes, sir," she said inaudibly. "Did you want to take a student? Cadet Abbot…"

"Cadet Abbot should stay here and apply herself," the headmaster said, and his look wasn't happy when he looked to Melina. She flushed a deeper red and suddenly found her tablet very interesting. All of the people around her did the same. "I need this one," he said, pointing to Anna. "Just for a moment."

Anna followed him out into the hallway. Under the glare of the station lighting, outside of the classroom's attempt at earthly light, he looked washed out. Not necessarily older, like when he'd been in the meeting with her mother, but faded.

"Cadet," he nodded. "Any word from your family?"

"Sir?"

"After your mother's visit."

"No, sir. I haven't talked to anyone since. I don't expect I'll have any word until the retrieval team returns and the trial begins."

"And you are okay with this?"

"Realities of Fleet life, Sir. I have a mission here and have to complete it."

He nodded. "Thank you, Cadet. I was just curious."

Anna was surprised. "If I may, Sir, why?"

The headmaster gave a little nervous laugh, just three quick notes. His pale face looked odd as he smiled. "It's always big news when your mother is involved, Cadet. I was just wondering if it meant something for the Academy."

"Oh," she said, watching the way he gave her a friendly look, almost embarrassed. "I don't know what will happen."

"Very well. You can return to class," he said, giving her a salute that she returned quickly.

"Thank you," she said, as he turned and walked away. Anna didn't know what to make of it. Days ago, she hadn't even seen the man outside of official pictures. She was sure he wasn't being honest with her, either. The nervous laugh and the way he acted seemed too perfect. He was faking and not telling her why he was asking. Or so her instincts told her. Growing up around her mother's shifty people had honed those skills.

Everyone, including the Captain, looked at her with faces full of questions as the door clicked back open and Anna stepped into the room. "I'm sorry, Professor," she said, using the more prestigious title. "Please continue."

Captain Stetler didn't know where she had been, Anna realized. She looked at her notes for a long moment, before turning and drawing a diagram of a typical cargo hold on the board. The rest of the class, the Captain didn't ask any questions, but lectured in a much quieter tone than usual.

Chapter 9

Anna was surprised when Melina stopped next to her table in the mess hall. Anna had her replacement tablet out, checking over her homework for the afternoon. It wasn't until the taller girl cleared her throat that Anna looked up.

"Oh, sorry," Anna said. "Want to sit?"

"Definitely not," Melina said. "I have a place," she said, with a look. Anna turned to see the rest of her crew, including some upperclass male cadets, all watching. "I wanted to know what that was about today."

"Are you being friendly just for information?" Anna asked. Melina just shrugged. "With the headmaster? He asked about my mom."

"Is she coming back?" Melina asked, some of the excitement slipping into her voice. Anna saw the light in Melina's eyes. Anna realized that this might be another path to popularity for Melina. Her grades weren't going to put her on a ship. Then Anna chided herself for being paranoid.

"I don't know. He just had a question about some stuff," Anna said.

"Oh. Be that way, then. That's why people don't like you, you know."

"Why's that?" Anna said. She felt the tingle in her hands that she knew meant she was getting angry. She'd spent a lot of time with therapists as a kid, learning not to hit.

"You have the most famous mother ever and you pretend you don't care. Everyone here would love to meet her and you blow us all off."

"I've met her, Melina. She's not that exciting."

Melina started to say something, then turned and stormed back to her table. Anna watched her reach the table and launch into some dramatic story, then turned back to her homework.

"Why do you let her get to you?"

Anna looked up to see her brother standing by the table, staring down some of the upperclass boys that were still looking over at Anna. "Don't start trouble, Steve."

"I arrived in the middle of trouble, sister," he said, pulling a seat out from the table. He was carrying a plastic-wrapped sandwich and a bottle of water. She smelled peanut butter as soon as he opened it and she had to smile.

"Such a macho lunch, my hero."

"PB&J has vital nutrients and vitamins," he said, between bites.

"So what are you doing here? Your lunch shift isn't for another half hour."

"Simulators finished early."

"That never happens. I don't know anyone who would give up a chance to pilot."

Steve took a napkin from her tray and wiped his face as the last of the sandwich disappeared. He took a moment to look over at Melina's table, giving a nasty look. "Mayberry set us up for dogfights with fighters today."

"Sounds like something you'd have to pry me out of with a crow bar."

"Not everyone loses as well as you."

Anna laughed. "I beat you more than you beat me, Sephalos."

"Not as I remember it. Either way, you'd have cleaned up this crowd. Mayberry changed my ship three times to limit me and I still beat them all in record time. Twice."

"Record time, Steve? Who keeps records?"

"I do. I declare it a record."

They both laughed. "When's the last time you didn't win?" Anna asked.

"In class? About two years ago, in that mixed ages tournament."

"I bet they can't wait to get you into a ship," Anna smiled.

"I hope," Steve said, then leaned back in his chair, pushing it a bit back from the table. Anna watched his face lose all the fun and she turned to see three of Melina's potential boyfriends walking towards them.

"What's up, guys?" Steve asked.

They stopped at the edge of the tale, all facing him. Anna knew their names from being around, but didn't really know them. "You got a problem?" one of them asked.

"My sister," Steve answered. Anna stuck out her tongue. Both of the twins laughed, briefly. Steve rotated his chair a bit, so he was facing them in the aisle a little more openly.

"You think you're pretty special, don't you? Showing off all the time, sucking up. You need to learn your place."

"Oh, good. Ritual hazing. I didn't have enough of this first year," Steve said, pushing the chair back a little more. He had his toes on the ground, rocking back a little as he faced them.

The talker pushed Steve's shoulder. The chair started to tip some more. Anna leapt to her feet.

One of the three grabbed her. And copped a feel as he did it, laughing in her ear. Her elbow connected just underneath his ribcage, hard enough to make her hand spasm. He grunted and let go of her breast, but hooked the other arm around her waist tighter.

Steve tipped, in slow motion to Anna's eyes. The two other upperclassman were already moving, waiting for him to fall. Except he didn't. His shoes squeaked as his toes slowed the slide, then he was moving forward.

The one that pushed him still had his arm out. Steve caught it in one hand and jerked the guy forward, punching him with a jab that was all momentum. Blood spurted from his busted nose as he stumbled out of the way. The second one took on a fighting stance and aimed a kick.

Steve grunted as the kick hit his back. He'd turned, still coming forward, taking the shot on the thickest part of his body. Then he snapped the other way, coming to a halt as his foot shot out in his own kick. He caught the upperclassman in the knee and the attacker went down with a startled cry.

"Did you just fondle my sister?"

"No, man," the third one said.

"He's lying, Steve, but don't worry."

"Okay," Sephalos said, sitting back down in his chair.

The third guy looked confused, as Anna turned back to see his face. Then she swung her head back. His nose didn't break, but she felt it bend and he howled. Both his hands were off her then. She pivoted, putting her fists into his bellybutton in rapid combination. His stomach was rock-hard muscle, but he wasn't prepared. He stumbled back, gasping.

"Not so grabby now, are you?" Anna asked, stepping away from the chair.

"You still want to fight, little girl?" he asked, sucking in air. He stood, probably taller than the other two, and took a ready position.

Anna mirrored his position. They circled, for just a moment, and then he lunged. His longer arms reached out, trying to grab her again. Anna let him get her by the shoulders. Then her left leg came up into his crotch. He started to drag her down as he fell, but she yanked his hands free.

He curled on the ground, tears in his eyes, his hands guarding his injury.

"Not bad," Ensign Mayberry said from the door. He was standing with a couple of other Security men. They looked a lot more serious than him, though. They even had stunners in hand.

"A lesson for you, Cadet," the ensign said, as he walked over to where Anna's opponent was down. "You wouldn't be so careless against a smaller man, but against a woman you were sloppy. I think you've learned not to differentiate in a fight, yes?"

He nodded, on the ground.

"A second lesson, Cadet," Ensign Mayberry said, kneeling down and putting a hand on the boy's shoulder. He spoke quietly. Anna could hear and she figured Steve might. "If you ever touch another cadet like that, without his or her permission, I'll kick you myself. Right into the brig."

The boy on the ground went a little whiter, but nodded. Security moved away from the door to allow a pair of academy medics in.

"Are you ok?" Ensign Mayberry asked Anna, then repeated the question with a cooler look to Steve. Both nodded.

"I'm not going to take a report right now, because experience has taught me neither of you will file one," Mayberry smiled. "But I'm sure someone will have a word with you soon."

"We're always happy to help Security with any investigation," Anna said. Steve laughed a little, hiding it with a drink from his bottle.

"I'd just advise you both to be careful. You're big fish in the pond of the academy, but there are people out there who could really damage you. Even one of these stupid bullies, if he thought first, could take someone your size."

"I know. That's why I don't fight fair," Anna told him. Mayberry smiled and Anna found herself really liking the bright smile and the way his eyes crinkled.

Chapter 10

"About time this day ended," Alicia said, tossing her uniform suit onto the floor as she pulled her running clothes out of a drawer.

"I know," Anna said to her roommate. "What made it long for you?"

"Typical first year stuff. You've been through it, I'm sure."

"Sure, but they put you with older students so we can help you deal with all of that."

Alicia smiled. "Older? You have the face of a ten year old, Anna. If it wasn't for that body, you'd be sent back to Earth on sight. Or you'd have to wear an ID badge all the time."

Anna laughed. "I look a lot like my mom did, I hear." She pulled her academy-issue shorts and tank top on, fidgeting them into place over academy issue underwear. Alicia always changed into civilian gear, but Anna liked to keep the idea going that she was aboard a long-haul mission without civilian gear.

"Is it true that she was here a few days ago?"

"Yeah, family stuff," Anna admitted. "I'm surprised the rumor mill hasn't been going more."

"That usually happen when she's here?"

"I hear it used to. She's only been here a few times since I started. And Steve."

"But more with your older brother?"

"Yeah, when he was here she was still active in the Fleet. That was quite a mess."

"How?"

"Family stuff. I can't say more. I shouldn't have mentioned it."

"Typical top secret answer. They warned me about that when they put me with a Cosgrove. Lets get to the track before it fills up."

They jogged the halls, dodging the occasional cadet in transit. Most had their noses in books or were juggling take out meals and homework. A few underclassmen said hi to Alicia and most gave wary nods to Anna.

"So how was your day? I never asked," Alicia said as they started the mile long loop that ran atop the classrooms. The deck was completely open, so they could see a few other knots of runners, solo or in clusters, around the giant room.

"Other than the fight you can't wait to ask about?"

"Yeah. I know you'll have to tell me."

"Ok. Things all just feel weird lately. People are weird. Waiting on some family stuff is weird. It's like it's a constant full moon."

"I'm from the moon, you know," Alicia said, with a shy smile.

"Sorry. But you know what I mean."

"Of course. We have a few people that get nutty when it's full Earth out of the dome." Anna smiled, not sure if she was joking.

The first quarter of a mile passed slowly, just getting warmed up. Anna liked to go slow, too, just to see who was on the track. Maybe a bad habit, but it was something she always remembered from Jeecey. Scouting the location was a way to stay safe.

"So you and your brother kicked some butt," Alicia said. She wasn't even breathing hard yet, despite their quickening pace on the first turn.

"They weren't expecting anyone to fight back."

"But what was it all about?"

"I don't know. Male macho stuff."

"But," Alicia started and Anna raised a hand. She stopped talking instantly.

The runner coming up behind them at an intersect trajectory was slowing to match them. She hadn't been able to get a good look before, so Anna wanted to listen and get ready.

"Evening, cadets," Ensign Mayberry said. He was in a tee shirt that could have been painted onto his muscles and shorts that ended midthigh, showing a lot of muscle.

"Hello, sir," Alicia said and Anna nodded. She was surprised by the little circle of ink on the outside of his right leg, closest to her.

"You a veteran?"

"Why do you ask, Cadet?" Mayberry said with a smile. Anna felt her face turning red, and it wasn't from the running. She was staring.

"Your tattoo."

"Oh, neat," Alicia said, almost coming to a stop. A pair of upperclass women gave them looks as the dodged past. "Sorry," she said, using her long legs to pick up speed again.

"All the staff are veterans, Cadet. You knew that."

"I guess so. You just seem so young. I thought maybe it was a first posting for superior service of something. I didn't expect combat."

"That wouldn't be a reward," Mayberry said. Alicia laughed. Then blushed.

"What was your posting?"

"Nothing as fun as this," he said as they turned into another straightaway. "Race you," he said, bursting away.

Anna gave it her best, but couldn't keep up with him. Alicia just tagged beside her. Anna was pretty sure she'd have been a match for Mayberry.

"That was the worst evasive answer ever, Ensign," Anna followed up as they met up on the first corner, where he was jogging at a cooling pace. She sucked in air, hoping she didn't sound too gaspy and weird.

Mayberry smiled. "I thought it was pretty clever. It's rare anything I say makes two pretty girls' hearts race."

Alicia giggled again. "That's borderline inappropriate, Ensign," Anna scowled.

"No, it was very inappropriate, Cadet. I apologize."

She couldn't tell if he was serious or not. Or even if she was serious in calling him on it. The trio ran together for the rest of the straightaway, to where a Security man in uniform waved at the Ensign.

"Enjoy your run, ladies. Work calls."

Anna nodded and Alicia giggled. They watched, until they hit the turn, as an animated conversation followed. Then both Security men bolted out of the room.

"What was that about?" Alicia said.

"Security business, I'm sure. I didn't know that other officer, though."

"That's not what I meant, Anna. Why were you so mean to him?"

"He's a grown man, Alicia. We're kids."

"He's like two years older than you, Anna. He was trying to flirt."

"He can try harder, then," she huffed.

They kept going, with just the slap of feet and occasional nods at other runners, until they reached the doors. Now Steve stood there, waving in a curt motion.

"Be right back," Anna said.

"I'll come," Alicia said quickly. Anna wasn't surprised to see her eyes lock onto the taller twin.

"What's up, Steve? You remember Alicia, right?"

Sephalos nodded absently. "Hi," he said. "Anna, those four Security ships all just departed. With two assault frigates that just docked about an hour ago."

"So it's happening?"

"What's happening?" Alicia asked, but both of the twins just shook their heads.

"Any word from mom or dad?"

"Nothing. They are keeping it dark."

"Thanks for letting me know. I'll let you know what I hear."

"Same here. Bye," he said, dodging back out of the track as fast as the Security men.

"You Cosgroves are so mysterious."

"I'm not a...yeah, you're pretty much right," Anna said, bending into a stretch. "I'm not feeling like running anymore. I'm going to get something to eat and take it home. Okay?"

"I'll finish up here," Alicia said, with a little smile. Anna was glad that the rookie was getting more perceptive. "Bye."

Anna walked to the mess, watching some of the guys give her looks that were leers and some that were fear. Mostly, though, she was wondering about the ships that had just left and what was happening to her brother.

Chapter 11

The marketplace was almost empty as the sun set. Weak light came from ancient electrical lights, where the solar collectors were dirt covered or just worn. Sergei liked the dark. He was wrapped in an old cloak he's taken from a clothesline someplace years ago, that was still too large for him. The dark wool was good for his blonde hair and pale skin, though. He was wrapped tight, with only his pale face showing and half of that covered with smudged dirt. Without it, he'd have glowed brighter than the streetlamps.

"Need something, wee one?" one of the vendors asked, and Serg smiled. The accent was exactly was he was looking for.

"Cavort?"

"You're a little young for that, ain't you?" the elderly woman said, leaning forward on a shaky stool to stare over her table of wares at the little boy.

"My money is old," he said, palming a credit note so it flashed slightly in the light. Then it disappeared back into the dark folds of the cloak.

"Who am I to deny the fun?" she asked, pulling a small bag from inside her patterned tunic. The bag was the same sort of fabric, worn thin. The whole affair smelled of unwashed body and something very musty, like moldy dirt.

"Get it local?" Serg asked, sliding the note across the table with a flick of his wrist. She scooped it up just as quickly and stowed it out of sight.

"Cousin of mine has a place in the Baker's Alley. Come around any time," she cackled. Serg nodded and pocketed the little bag.

Four stalls over, Gannar fell in line behind him. He was dressed in another large cloak, but this one much cleaner. His face was uncovered, but he was wearing goggles that had the faint glow of tech. Neither said anything, but just wound there way through the maze of stalls until the smell of bread filled the air.

"Not fair. I haven't eaten all day," Serg said.

"I saw you eat two bowls of soup not an hour ago."

"Sure, for nutrition. Nothing good like this," the little brother said, throwing back his hood. He took a bite of a roll the size of his hand that he'd pocketed off one of the tables.

"Not smart, kid. You're carrying Cavort and stealing?"

"What are they going to do? Carry me off to the jail that doesn't exist anymore since someone blew the entire back wall off it?"

"I told you that half a pound was all the explosive I needed."

"And I told you that a pound was going to make a statement."

"That statement being the police shouldn't come into the alleys anymore?"

"Of course," Serg grinned, finishing the roll. "As for the Cavort," he said, opening the fabric bag and sniffing. "It's real," he nodded, then dropped the brown powder into the gutter.

"You know from the smell?"

"Something like that," Serg said. Gannar stared for a moment, then shook his head. "So which baker do we visit?"

Gannar was quiet a moment, studying the alley. "Probably the one with those armed guards."

"My guess, too," his little brother said, pulling his hood back up. "Let's go see about stealing us some drug-production equipment."

"We just need the heat transfer mechanism. I don't care about the rest of it."

"Sure, but what fun is it to say we're going to steal stolen ship parts back again? A sense of adventure, big brother, requires the proper ability to describe."

Gannar laughed and followed the dark little shape into the alley.

Chapter 12

Alicia screamed.

Anna sat bolt upright, reaching for the flashlight she kept next to the bed. Then she froze as she took in the scene around her.

"Be very still, Cadet," one of the men in the helmets said, his voice distorted by the mask. He had Lieutenant's bars on the chest of the suit.

She looked over. Alicia was sitting up in bed, the sheets clutched around her armpits. Another of the black-suited soldiers had a hand over her mouth and was holding a stunner to her side.

"I'm being very still," Anna repeated. The guns aimed at her weren't stunners. She didn't think any sort of threat allowed for the use of projectile weapons aboard a space station. The risk of explosion was high enough, even before the risk of someone shooting a hole in the side of the academy was raised. But the wide barrels pointed at her definitely were projectile guns. Of the scary sort.

"On your feet," the officer said. Two other armed people in uniform stood at the open door, targeting her. Anna took in for the first time that all the lights were on in her room, spilling out in the dark hall.

Anna slid out of bed, pulling her pajama pantlegs down as she moved. One of the rifles twitched as she bent to pull her slippers on. "It's cold, ok?" she said as she stood, hugging herself. The tank top was good for sleeping under covers, but not much for being yanked from under them.

"Got a robe?" the officer asked. Anna pointed at the door. The officer moved over to pull it off the hook, jamming hands into the deep pockets and tossing some tissues and a hair tie onto the desk. Then it was tossed at her, in a low arc that made it easy to Anna to catch it without moving dangerously.

"Thank you," Anna said, pulling it over the thin pajamas. It didn't stop all of the chills, but she felt better.

"Now move," the voice said. Anna walked slowly, keeping her hands visible. The officer turned to let her pass, then fell in behind. As she got close, Anna noticed the officer wasn't much taller than her. A woman, maybe. That would explain letting her keep some dignity before being marched away.

The brig was a tiny little section of the Security office, which was already fairly small considering the relative size of the station. Anna waited as two of the armed men went into the room, running sweepers for any electronics, and then herded her into the chair. The smaller officer followed a second later, taking off her helmet to reveal a large bun of blonde hair and bright blue eyes.

"Do you know why you're here, Cadet?" the Security officer said. She holstered her pistol with a series of clicks that meant the no one without her DNA would be drawing the weapon.

"Because you told me to come here," Anna responded. She settled back into the chair, trying to find the comfortable way to sit. It wasn't easy, but she knew that's why the chairs had been picked. The trick was to avoid being so antsy you'd answer the wrong questions.

"Apart from that."

"No, ma'am."

The door clicked open again and Anna turned, then jumped up. Two people entered in a blur of fancy uniforms. Her father hugged her and she felt a little kiss on the top of her head.

"Colonel, Admiral," the Lieutenant greeted. Anna felt her father look away, maybe giving the officer a raised eyebrow about the order of her greetings, but he didn't say anything.

Stavros Stanis Wroclaw was a skeletal figure often compared to the Grim Reaper by people that only knew him from photographs or at a distance. He was six and a half feet tall and barely two hundred pounds. His olive skin was pulled tight over sharp cheekbones where not buried by a beard and mustache of thick, jet black hair.

"Thank you, Admiral, for joining us," the security Colonel said. Another woman, Anna heard. She looked up to see a face that was quite similar to her father. This woman was the same Mediterranean olive, with sharp black eyes. She wasn't armed like her security staff, but looked just as dangerous in the shipside uniform of Fleet Security.

"Colonel Depopolos, it is good to see you again. I trust the fact I recommended you to the academy is why I am here and not Admiral Cosgrove?"

She didn't flinch at all. Not at Admiral Wroclaw's tone, which was friendly and kind. The mention of Admiral Cosgrove frequently made Security wince.

"Actually, Sir, it was because you were already in orbit and could be summoned here quickly. It would take an additional three hours for Admiral Cosgrove to arrive."

"Well, then, what couldn't wait?"

"Sir, in order to question a minor, we need a parent present in some cases. Given the sensitive nature of what is going on, we felt it important to have you present. This is to advise you," she said, drawing a piece of paper from a thin case she'd set on the table, "that you are not present in a professional or counsel position, although you have the right to request counsel for your child and yourself."

"I'm an engineer, not a lawyer. Why don't you tell me what this is about?"

"Cadet, are you in contact with a man named Gannar Charles Trilouis?"

"No, I am not," Anna said quickly. She was surprised by the question, but it wasn't the first time.

"Have you spoken with him in the last month?"

"I have not spoken with him in almost two years."

"When was the last time you spoke with him?"

"Aboard this station, in the staff simulator bay, almost two years ago."

"We have reviewed the footage of that encounter. You seemed close," the Colonel said, glancing up from her notes to fix Anna with the dark eyes.

"He's my brother."

"Half-brother, correct?"

"Yes."

"Can I ask where this is going, Colonel?" Admiral Wroclaw said. Still in that kind voice, but with a certain authority to it. "This is not only old news, but well-covered old news."

"Just a couple more questions, please. Cadet, were you aware an action was being taken to arrest Mr. Trilous?"

"Yes. My mother told me. I believe there should be footage of her visit."

"Did you communicate this in any way to any person?"

"No," Anna said. She met the Colonel's eyes as she talked. Anna was surprised that the look wasn't the cold look she expected from Security after all those other interviews.

"Very well. Lieutenant Morales will take you to temporary quarters, Cadet."

"Why not her own?" her father asked, as Anna started to say the same thing.

"Unfortunately, we can't allow contact with the student population while an investigation is ongoing."

"And what is that investigation?"

"I cannot disclose that at this time," the colonel said, a little embarrassed. "I'm sorry, Admiral."

"It's ok, Dad. I'll tell you. Jeecey got away and they think we tipped him off."

"Why do you say that?" the Colonel asked, the laser eyes back in full effect. Much more the hard look of professional Security.

"It's the logical end of those questions you were asking."

"Lt. Morales, please," the Colonel said, pointing. There was a mechanical noise as the officer put her helmet back in place, unholstering the weapon. Anna stood, following instructions again as they marched her away.

Chapter 13

Steve nodded as his father entered the room, trailed by a Fleet Security officer in shipside uniform. Someone important to be pulled from a Fleet ship instead of a ground base, he reasoned.

"Sephalos, I am Colonel Depopolos. I have some questions to ask you. We have asked your father to be here because you are a minor. Do you have any questions or anything to say?"

"No," Steve said, drawing tighter into the chair. The colonel's eyebrows twitched a little at his expression, so he tried to go blank again.

"Cadet, are you in contact with Gannar Charles Trilouis?"

Steve laughed. It felt good, as all the butterflies in his stomach suddenly disappeared. "My brother? Not in years."

"What is funny?"

"That's not why I thought you were here."

"Why would you think Security would be talking to you, Steve?" the Colonel said. Her voice was soft and friendly. Steve didn't believe it at all, because her eyes were just as wary. No one that watched so closely for a tic or twitch was being friendly.

"Nothing. Just me being silly."

"Sephalos, please cooperate," his father said. Steve turned to frown at the tall man, sitting backwards on a chair over his shoulder.

"Our tablets were acting up. I thought maybe it was about hacking school supplies."

"Everyone does that. Everyone smart, anyway," the Admiral said when the Colonel went to say something.

"Yes, that's what I was going to say. Anything else, Steve?"

"Well, maybe me and Josette?"

"Fraternization is frowned upon, but not illegal," the Admiral said again. "Unless your mother finds out," he finished, quietly. Steve had to smile at that.

"I think that will be irrelevant, but we will follow up," the Colonel said. "But for the matter at hand. You are certain you have not had contact with Gannar Trilouis?"

"No, ma'am. Er, yes, ma'am. I have not had contact with him. We didn't even talk much when we lived together."

"As my records indicate," she said, which Steve saw draw a raised eyebrow from his father. The admiral had moved a little closer as the exchange kept going. "Sephalos, do you know this boy?"

She held out a black and white printout. It was fairly grainy. A surveillance shot from some sort of automated camera, Steve was pretty sure. Nothing that Fleet Security would be using. All he could make out was the boy was small and pale. His face was close to the camera and the background was mostly a blur.

"No idea who he is."

"You are certain?"

"No question, ma'am."

She slid the picture back into the case, which she snapped shut. Automated locks kept clicking as she rested her hand on top of it and stared at Steve. "I'm going to ask that you be held in private quarters for a day or so. It's for your own safety, so that you can be watched without the rumor mill spiraling."

"I can't help but notice you didn't say the same thing to," the admiral started, but the security officer raised a hand.

"I'd prefer to keep things completely separate."

"You can't talk about one suspect in front of another, Dad," Steve said. "Sorry, Colonel. Fleet Command isn't as up on this as Fleet Security."

The Colonel returned the wry smile. Steve was impressed that it was an almost perfect mimic of his own look. "Fleet Security is well aware of your various connections, Cadet. Which is why you'll be in staff quarters instead of the brig for the next two days."

"Understood," Steve said, with a salute as he stood up.

"I'll be along in a moment to speak with you," his father said, and

Steve nodded, turning to where the Security officers were already waiting at the door.

"Are these my personal detachment?" Steve asked, pointing at the guards that had also led him to the room.

"I would suggest your levity is out of place."

"Just curious if they are a protection detail as well as a detainment detail, Colonel."

"Why would you ask that?" Admiral Wroclaw questioned.

"Just things I've observed," Steve said, walking out of the room.

The Admiral watched the younger officer's face for a moment. "Why did he ask that, Colonel?"

"I'd suggest your son has an active sense of humor."

"I'd disagree, as would you if you'd read his report. And I know you are thorough enough to have done so."

Colonel Depopolos sighed. "We do not believe there is an active threat."

"Then why does my fifteen year old son think there is? And call you on it?"

"If someone within the Fleet is aiding this fugitive, some might consider the closest relatives a threat. A way to get at or control him."

"That doesn't make sense. What aren't you telling me?"

"I'm not authorized to discuss this, Sir."

"I'm authorizing you, Colonel."

She paused, just for a moment. "There was verified intelligence, some months ago. Certain factions of radicals had indicated that this fugitive's ongoing escape was likely part of a high-ranking conspiracy within the Fleet. They threatened action against the family if an arrest was not made. Some interests very much want Mr. Trilouis to remain free."

"I did not hear of this."

"It was not released beyond a certain clearance level."

"It involves my children. It was released to them."

"No, Sir. It wasn't released to anyone outside the Fleet Command, except..."

Admiral Wroclaw read the nervous look on her face, knowing it was a look he'd probably made a few times in his life. "Except for a certain retired Admiral."

"Yes, sir. I don't know whether she discussed it with them or whether they found out through other means. I am not authorized to inquire into that. I can only report what Sephalos said."

"Please do. You can leave out our discussion, if you'd like."

"Thank you, Sir. But I would prefer to be accurate in my accounting."

"So who threatens my children, Colonel?"

"We never made any arrests, Sir. Suspicion indicates it may have been some senior shipboard officers. All we have is rumors."

"And very high security?"

"Yes, Sir. You have my promise."

"Thank you, Colonel. You are doing very well in your job."

She saluted and he returned it with his typical precision.

"Just be very careful how you proceed, Colonel," the Admiral said as he left the room, his own guard falling in behind him outside the door.

Chapter 14

Anna slumped on her bed, slapping the tablet down next to her.

"I'm bored," she announced to the empty room and had just the response she expected. More silence. Aside from a little hum from the engine room, much nearer the staff section than the dorms, it was perfectly still.

She picked up the tablet again, looking at the homework that had been forwarded to her. Gates had done the first draft of Nav problems and sent them to her. Goerlitz hadn't sent anything, but that didn't really surprise her. Emma's attitude had been bad lately and Anna not showing for class hadn't helped, she was certain.

Anna went to the door and knocked. She heard shuffling on the outside and then it slid open. Two large men in Security uniforms stood outside. They had stunners instead of heavy weapons, she was glad to see. She didn't know if that meant the threat had been downgraded, but it was one less thing to worry her.

"Can I go to the gym or something?"

"Confined to quarters mean just this room, Cadet," the taller one said.

"In my quarters, I'd have something to do."

"You have a tablet."

"It's a replacement. All it does is access my schoolwork."

"Then you have something to do," the female lieutenant called from down the hallway. Anna leaned forward and peeked out. Morales had set up a little desk and chair and was tapping away on a tablet just out of sight.

"Can someone at least bring me a change of clothes? So I can shower?"

"You can shower and put those back on."

"I'd like some underwear."

"An officer should be prepared to do with some temporary hardship."

Anna stepped back and let the door shut without another comment. She thought she heard some brief conversation in the hallway, probably laughing at her, but then it was back to silence as the locks clicked back into place.

"Ok. Let's do inventory," she said to herself. "One cotton tank top. One pair of cotton pants. One cotton robe. Two socks. Rubber soled slippers." She looked around at everything else in the room, which was mainly bolted down in shipboard fashion. "Two sheets, a blanket and a tablet."

"Not what you'd use to escape, is it? Ideally, I mean," a little voice called out.

Anna jumped, then looked around. She edged closer to the bed, looking at the tablet. The nav problems were gone. The starfield background was in place, but a small corner was filled with a grainy image. It moved with jerks and starts, like the camera wasn't quite tuned right.

"Who are you?"

"I would have thought 'how' would be the primary question. Seeking escape and all."

"I'm not trying to escape. I was just practicing."

"So you'll wait here until someone kills you?"

She sat on the bed, looking down at the face. The quality was so bad she couldn't see much other than a pale and round face. Maybe younger than her, to judge by the high voice, but the sound quality was so bad she couldn't tell. "Kills me? They are just being cautious."

"Of course they are, Cadet. It's totally not a way to segregate you until an accident happens."

"What sort of accident, since you know so much?"

"Oh, I imagine they'll offer to let you go back to get something and you just will take a wrong turn at an airlock. Wouldn't be the first time."

"You're nuts."

"Angela Pirrou. Linus Webster. Alastair Knight-Woodley. Just to name the ones I've read the files on."

"And who were they?"

"Cadets that knew too much, Anna. Follow along. I had been assured you were smart."

"And what is it I know?"

"A young man you refer to as Jeecey. Which is the stupidest nickname ever."

"What about my brother?" she said through clenched teeth. She kept hearing footsteps she knew weren't really there, like someone was getting ready to come in. Her mind kept hearing the locks start to click and she jumped a little every time she expected the noise.

"You're awfully possessive now that he's gone," the tinny voice said after a long pause.

"Answer me."

"I would have thought you'd been briefed on this. Your brother was."

"Gannar was?"

"And you're supposed to be the smart one? No, Sephalos. He knows. I thought he'd have told you."

"You aren't making sense."

"You are dense. Listen, there are people coming down the hall. Be careful until we find a way to get back in contact."

"Like this magic tablet thing isn't enough?"

"Don't ask stupid questions. We can only do this once before they catch on, now that they have your personal tablet. Just be careful," the little voice said. Then the screen flickered, back to her Nav homework.

Anna jumped as the door locks clicked. She pulled her robe tighter and almost laughed as the door slid open to show Melina Abbot standing with the woman Security officer.

"We decided you could go for a run. Cadet Abbot volunteered to accompany you."

"I don't have my stuff. Thank you, I mean," she said quickly.

"Cadet Abbot will take you to the staff gym, which is a direct route from here. I'll send someone to get your gear," the lieutenant said.

"Thanks," Anna said. "I mean, thank you, ma'am."

The officer just nodded. "Get moving. We can't dawdle."

"Thanks, Melina," Anna said as they started down the cool metal walkways. If anything, the staff section was even more Spartan than the student areas. There weren't any hangings on the walls or decorations. There weren't even designations about levels or other identifiers. Just plain metal walls, sometimes painted white, but mostly dull grey.

"Not a problem. I had to know what's going on."

"So everyone will have to talk to you?"

She laughed. "You're funny, Anna. Everyone already talks to me."

Anna laughed too. It was hard not to, even when Melina was annoying. "So you're just being nice?"

"I'm a lot nicer than you think, Anna. Just because we don't always get along doesn't mean it's all because I'm a bad person."

Anna nodded. "You're right, I suppose. I'm sorry."

"It's ok, Anna. So what is going on with you?"

"Something with my brother."

"The one you mentioned the other day? The older one?"

"Yeah. I don't really know what's up, though."

"Oh," she said. Anna imagined she was seeing all sorts of great gossip disappear before her eyes. "Hey, were you serious about the formal? Going with me, I mean?"

"If you want to, sure. As long as you don't get fresh with me," she smiled.

Melina flushed. "I told you, I'm not into girls."

"I was teasing you. You get embarrassed so easily. Guilty conscience?"

"That's not nice," Melina said, with a pout that almost made Anna laugh. She would have, if it hadn't been clear she was serious despite trying to make it look like a joke.

"Sorry, Melina. It's hard not to push your buttons."

"It's ok," Melina said, stopping at one of the junctions where four hallways met. "You know the way?"

"Not really. Left, I think," Anna said.

They turned down the metal walkways, listening to their feet echo. Anna slowed, thinking she was hearing another set of feet but not sure if it was just an echo because the place was so empty. She thought back to all the locks she'd thought she heard during the conversation, knowing her imagination was wild. But she also couldn't stop thinking about what the scratchy voice had told her.

Both of them jumped when something echoed as it hit the metal floor.

"What was that?" Anna asked.

"Someone dropped something. The staff does live here," Melina said, but Anna was pretty sure she was just convincing herself. Melina looked back down the hallway, to the four corners, but her eyes twitched back to Anna as they waited.

"But we haven't seen anyone. Everyone should either be at station or at work. It's the middle of the night."

"Sure, but it's the middle of the waking hour for some people that work nights, right?"

"Right," Anna said. "We're just jumpy." Anna looked down the hallway, and then back the way they'd came. The lights were set to a nighttime setting so that the halls were darker than previous times she'd been in the crew quarters. Shadows reached out from doorways all around them, grown menacing by the few dim lights.

"You'd think there's be people going to the canteen or the gym or something, right?" Anna asked. "Let's just wait a moment. Someone will show us the way to the gym."

"Okay. Just to humor you," Melina joked. They slid together into an alcove where a series of plugs showed one of the old communication devices had been there. It was big enough for the two of them to fit, their backs to the wall and deep enough that they were covered in shadows.

Anna heard her heart beating in the quiet of the hall, with Melina's echoing. They looked at each other and smiled a little. A moment later, the footsteps were clear. There weren't many other noises, other than the hum of the engines and the lower noise of the faint lights. A single person, moving fast.

"What do we do?" Melina hissed. Anna raised a finger to be quiet.

The security lieutenant went by, faster and quicker than they'd expected. Anna fought to contain a little noise and Melina gasped. She was moving so fast she was gone before she could hear it, though.

"Is she after us?" Melina asked. "We should tell her."

"Let's just get to the gym. If she's looking for us, we'll meet here there."

"I feel silly, Anna. She's Security."

"I know. I'm just being paranoid."

"Ok. Paranoid it is. So we should take another route? To make sure she doesn't see us dawdling?"

Anna thought about it. The hallway looked even darker from the cubbyhole. "Yes. Then we can also tell her we missed her passing us."

"Right," Melina said, looking at all of the metal walkways that spanned the inside of the station. "But how?"

"Fastest way would be across the engine deck and through the flight deck. If your reputation can handle it."

"Just keep your hands to yourself," Melina whispered with a glare, stepping out and grabbing the nearest ladder.

Anna followed a moment later, making sure the hall was empty, then scrambling up behind her new friend.

Chapter 15

Morris was angry. Steve could tell because the usually-still vein in his forehead was standing out and throbbing.

"Where is she?"

"I honestly don't know, Sir. I've been here by myself."

Morris went quiet. Steve wondered if the respectful tone had surprised him.

There was a series of clicks and the door to the room opened. It was the same grey walls on the outside. Ensign Mayberry stood there, now dressed in a tactical suit and carrying a sidearm.

"Team A is ready, Sir."

"Sephalos, I am very concerned about this threat. We're going to comb every inch of this station and find where your sister went. To be clear, I don't think anything has harmed her. Probably a misunderstanding," he said, frowning when Steve raised his eyebrows to question. "But we're making sure you're safe. You're going on a shuttle with a Security team in tight orbit."

"So someone on a capital ship can shoot us down?"

"Tight orbit, son," Morris corrected with a fairly friendly tone. Steve was as surprised by that as the term of endearment. "You'll be so close to the academy no one will pick you out as a separate ship."

"Has my father been informed?"

"We sent a message and dispatched a courier moments ago. Within the hour he'll have someone knocking on his door."

"Just in case someone is censoring his messages? Are you paranoid or is this a far-reaching plot?" Steve tried to give a little smile when he said it, to convey some sort of respect, but Morris stayed blank.

"Hopefully the former, Cadet," Morris said, pointing out the door. He picked up the replacement tablet and put it into a travel case, locking the electronic seals. "I'm sending this in a different direction, to throw anyone off for now."

Sephalos nodded to Mayberry and the three other men in tactical suits as he exited the room. A few techs and night shift staffers gave them odd looks, but didn't say anything. There was usually something weird in the academy, Steve figured.

The guy in the lead was cautiously scanning down each hall and looking around corners with his hand on his sidearm, Steve noted after the first corner. They thought something was up. A little finger of fear for Anna ran down his back as he thought of her. Especially as they entered the flight deck, giant rooms larger than a house full of dark spaces and heavy machinery. The whole room was empty, with their footsteps echoing around the huge space.

"I trust an AR-14 would be acceptable?" Mayberry said, pointing to one of the ships that was hooked into the fueling lines. Bright lights flashed across the hull as the computers hummed and ran their preflight checks.

Steve looked it over in surprise. It was a ten man ship, built for speed but capable of carrying the small crew in relative comfort for some weeks. Turret-mounted weapons pointed forward and back. There was no question it was a warship, on a small scale.

"I didn't know they'd been in full production."

"Your dad may have a secret or two he doesn't share," Mayberry laughed. "His shipyards have been turning out a few at a time for testing purposes."

"You know I...," Steve started.

"That you designed the control interface and played a large role in overall look?"

Steve laughed. He didn't know why. Maybe it was the way the four soldiers nodded seriously as Mayberry spoke. They were acknowledging his work.

"Yes, we are aware that this is a very user-friendly and pretty ship, Cadet. Now let's get it into space."

The inside was as nice as Steve remembered from the drawings. A little more plain than the artistic renderings, with grey cloth seats four deep in two rows behind the pilot and navigator chairs. Beyond that would be two bunk rooms and shower facilities. Storage was a variety of lockers along the walls and floor. It smelled new.

"Have a seat," Mayberry said, pointing out a chair right behind the pilot. Mayberry slid into the pilot seat, stowing his sidearm in a little alcove by the chair as he strapped in. Outside, the other three members unhooked the fuel lines and did the exterior parts of the test. Mayberry was silent as he clicked buttons and checked gauges, before turning with a smile.

"We're good to go. If things go as planned, maybe you can pilot it back into the base."

Steve grinned and felt like a fool. He knew he looked like an idiot, like a little kid being offered candy and not being able to say no. "That'd be great," he said, knowing it was a huge rules violation.

The other men climbed aboard. The last one in hit a few buttons and the sound of the pressure lock filled the cabin for a moment. "That's something we need to revise," he laughed, taking a seat near the back.

Steve laughed too. All of them were young, not more than five years older than him. One was black and another indeterminately ethnic, but they all looked alike with the short hair and black tactical suits.

The engine roar shook the cabin and Steve leaned forward to look out the cabin window. The hatch door opened a fraction of its full width, but it was enough for Mayberry to easily glide free of the station. Steve wished for a side window, to see the outside of the station. Very few cadets ever got to look at the outside of the academy before senior year, when they took shuttles out of the flight deck. They all knew how to fly shuttles before starting school, but that was on Earth. Security concerns kept everyone inside most of the time.

"Command One, this is Team A," Mayberry said. "Advise."

There was a crackle of static and Morris boomed through the cabin. "Team A, proceed."

"Will do, Sir. Over," Mayberry said, then turned the knob on the radio. The whole panel went dark and Steve leaned back in surprise.

"Fleet Reg 432.32 says communications systems are to remain in a powered state at all times, right?" the black Security man asked.

"Yes, sir," Steve answered.

"Except?" he prompted.

"Except? Missions of absolute secrecy and at times when safety requires such action."

"Do you not feel safe?" he asked.

Steve felt a little sweat on the small of his back. "No, I feel quite safe."

"Meaning?"

He thought, longer than usual but the stares of the four guards made him nervous. "A mission of absolute secrecy?"

"Do you get along with your half-brother, Sephalos?" Mayberry asked, turning the pilot's chair to look back. Out of the window, there was just spotty blackness as they floated away from the station.

"I don't bear him any ill will, if that's what you mean."

"Do you think he's a traitor?" the other white one asked. The only one with a patch on the tactical suit showing a name. Ensign Sunderland, bearing the patch of the carrier Io.

"I think he's very confused and he made stupid decisions that have blown up in his face."

Steve watched their faces as he talked. Mayberry frowned a little while the black man smiled a little. Sunderland stared at him with soft brown eyes that were disconcerting given the severity of his expression. He couldn't see the other one, because he'd moved to the nav chair and was facing the map computer. The glow of the screen reflected out, but Steve couldn't see details of the charts in the reflection.

"Our mission is relatively simple, Cadet. We find him and bring him back for a trial. He gets to explain himself. He doesn't mysteriously die in flight or get a summary execution in the field."

"And if I'd said I hated my brother?" Steve asked, regretting it as soon as the words crossed his brain.

Mayberry laughed. All of the others joined in after a moment. "You are with us for a reason, Cadet. You have all of the skills we do. You know the target better. You're here as a full member of our team. No joke. No BS."

"Why would Morris authorize this?"

"Morris didn't," the black one said. He pulled aside the vest on his tacticals to show his uniform jacket underneath. "Morris" was emblazoned in the standard black thread. "This comes from up high, not from my uncle."

"How high?" Steve asked, having a guess at the answer.

"Richard here isn't the only one with family in the service, is he?" Mayberry asked, spinning his chair around without waiting for an answer.

"We're going, regardless of what I say?"

"You're almost an officer. You value the protection of our home and the work of the Fleet. I know what you're going to say." Mayberry said this without looking back, as he strapped in and punched in the codes the navigator was showing him.

"I get a tactical suit, right?"

"I knew he'd say that," Mayberry laughed, as he punched the throttle to full power.

Chapter 16

Anna watched from the giant glass windows as a single ship launched and floated outside the academy's bays.

"What is it?" Melina whispered in her ear.

"That ship design just surprised me. I didn't think they'd made any yet."

"I don't know what you're talking about," Melina said. "Come on." She edged forward, staying in the shadow but near enough the window not to fall into a waste pit or a fuel tank. Anna followed a few feet behind, always watching the edges of the room for any movement. The bays were dead silent, other than the ship that had just left. That made Anna feel odd, but she didn't know why. Nerves, she suspected. Anything out of the ordinary just looked weird right now.

"Last ladder," Melina said, hauling herself up in a few jumps. Anna waited until she was up, then followed just a hair slower.

"You know the way well," Anna teased. She was surprised that Melina looked surprised and hurt at first, before smiling. "Sorry, I didn't mean anything."

"No, it's ok. Yeah, I've been here with a guy before. It's nice to get some privacy from it all."

"Is it worth risking suspension?"

"What, you've never been up here?"

"For class, or with my mom. Not for...you know. Boys."

"Or girls?"

"Quit teasing."

Melina smirked, moving down the last catwalk. Anna followed, toward the glowing light leaking from around the edges of a door set in the wall. Then the door popped open with a fast series of clicks and the lieutenant stepped out, sidearm drawn.

"Please stand still," she said, very quietly.

"Yes ma'am!" Melina said, throwing her arms in the air.

"No one talk. I need to get Anna someplace safe. The situation has changed."

Anna felt the butterflies in her stomach again. She watched the lieutenant, standing next to the door, and Melina frozen in place between them. The lieutenant's face looked scary as she peered into the dark room and the gun in her hand was scarier. Anna recognized it as a standard service pistol. She'd fired one herself, hundreds of time before even signing up for the academy. She'd just never been on this side of it before.

Anna jumped. The hole seemed huge until she hit it, bouncing off the side as she fell back down.

"Ahh!" she yelled out as she caught the rungs of the ladder.

Stopping so fast made her head spin, but before she could recover her legs had taken over. She jumped down the last few feet and sprinted into the open bays.

"Anna, wait!" she heard Melina call behind her. She didn't. She slalomed around the parked ships. She kept jumping each time the shiny metal hulls sent her reflection back into her face.

"Anna!" she heard another voice. She spun, trying to pick it out. Gates was deep in the shadows, only visible because he held a tiny penlight that waved at her.

She ran towards him. "I don't know," she started to say, when she realized it wasn't a penlight. It was the targeting scope of a night-equipped service pistol. She tried to stop. Anna felt a pain as she kicked herself in the ankle, stopping so short and pitched forward. Her shoulder popped as she piled into his thick legs.

Gates fell on top of her as she landed, skidding across the floor. He was heavy. She reached for the pistol, laying on the ground, but he was fast.

"Move, fast," he ordered. He stood. He didn't aim at her.

The pistol shot filled the empty area. Gates dove to the ground, staring at where the wall above his head had buckled and burnt. Little pieces of metal pinged to the ground. "Move, fast," he repeated, pushing her.

Anna crawled. Faster than she'd crawled before. The obstacle courses at cadet training weren't anything like the pressure she felt. She felt Gates right behind her. She turned to look once and all she saw was a big hand, pushing her forward. He hit her butt and she started to complain before she heard the footsteps running up above on the walkways.

She fell onto her elbows as the big hand grabbed her ankle and pulled her to a stop. She shuffled back, trying to stay balanced on her hands and knees as she ducked as low as she could be.

"Trap door, eighteen feet ahead," Gates said quietly. Then he turned and looked through the scope, at the walkways above. "Go!"

Anna started moving. She shuffled her hands and feet as fast as she could, feeling the burn as her pajamas tore and her skin was scraped by the metal floor. The trap door was where he said, a little square of pale light on the floor. She crawled onto the square, looking all around for a keypad or some sort of lock.

It was moving. Anna started, almost falling backwards. There were cables she hadn't seen on two sides, connected to giant pulleys. She looked for the floor, but it was too dark to tell how far away it was. Two shots rang out, on opposite sides of the bay, just as the freight elevator clicked into place on the bottom of a ship. Anna scrambled to the side, off the square before it moved again, and waited. Either it was very quiet outside or the ship was very insulated.

She scuttled forward, bumping into boxes in the dark. It took a moment to find the wall, and another few minutes to find one of the little windows she knew were always there on Fleet ships. It was behind a giant crate and she would have missed it if there wasn't a bright yellow flash.

"What was that?" she asked herself, quietly. Just to hear someone's voice. She couldn't get all the way behind the crate and it was too big to move, but she could lean against it and peer at the window.

The yellow had been the launch rockets. Now there was a metal tower fading quickly into the distance, some part of the academy. She was in space.

Chapter 17

The AR-14 didn't have a mirror. One of the bunkroom cupboards was some shiny surface that was supposed to be reflective enough for fixing hair or arranging uniforms. Sephalos understood the logic behind it, as the ship was built for combat. Still, putting the long sleeves of his jacket into place would have been much more fun, he smiled, if he'd been able to see it.

"Natural fit," Morris said. He'd shrugged off his own jacket, revealing a uniform shirt marked with the logo of Fleet Command. It was the third different unit he'd seen marked on this crew. Morris watched as Steve pulled the last pieces of the tactical suit into place.

"Thank you. It does feel good," Steve said, stretching and flexing. It was heavier than cloth, no question, but not as weighty as he'd expected.

"We don't have a name patch or anything for you. I hope that's ok."

Steve looked at the shoulder and at the blank stripe on the chest. "I sort of like it this way."

"The unknown commando?"

"A slate to be written upon," Steve said back.

"I like that. I really do. You're a man that's not going to let family tell you who you are supposed to be, are you?"

"Speaking from experience?"

"Not at all. I'm an enlisted man from the middle of nowhere. I was lucky to make Sergeant. Then my dad's long lost brother turned out to not be so lost and he got me a new job. I'm grateful for having the coattails to ride. But I'm riding away from a lot, you know?"

Steve nodded. "Everything in my life is based around what my mom did or what my older brother did. I like that what happened before helps me open doors, but I'm ready to be myself."

"That's what I like to hear," Sunderland said, coming up from the trap door in the floor. He carried a familiar looking black box that he sat on one of the bunks and opened with a series of taps onto a black keypad.

Sunderland drew out two stunners, brand new with security tags still in place. He broke off the tags, throwing them with a smile, and clicked the power pack into place with a delicate touch.

"Pretend we told you to be careful," he said, holding one by the barrel and offering it over.

"Sir, I'm not cleared..."

"You're a part of Team A, aren't you? Then you need to carry at least a stunner."

"Sir," Steve smiled, taking the pistol grip. The metal was a little

warm from the battery in the handle. He spun the control switches on the grip, rolling the little wheels with his left thumb. The gauges on the side of the weapon dipped or lit as he moved.

"Holster it before you shoot yourself," Morris said. Steve laughed but complied.

"This is going to be your briefing, so pay attention," Ensign Sunderland said, sitting down on one of the bunks. Steve nodded quickly and took a seat. Morris, already sitting on the floor, leaned back a little more and stretched out his long legs.

"What's our mission?" the ensign asked.

"Arrest and return Gannar Trilouis."

"How do we do that?"

Steve's eyes grew big. It felt like a week as the two of them watched him. "I honestly don't know," Steve answered.

They both laughed, a little. "Don't worry. That's not the million dollar question that you're here to answer," Sunderland said.

"We do it by listening to the chatter, collecting good information and coming in with a small, precise team," Morris said. "Chatter indicates he's surprisingly close to the frontier, on a little world called Euphrates. Spies on the ground have seen suspicious persons who could be our man."

"And then we bring the team. Ensign Mayberry is our pilot.

Sergeant Morris and Airman Lao are combat veterans. I'm a Security specialist with extradition training. And you know what Team A also has?"

"A stunningly gorgeous computer nerd?" Steve said. He laughed when he said it, but he felt the nerves. He knew they were buttering him up, or sucking up. Maybe they wanted him to like them. Maybe there was something else. Too many years of being played always made him nervous.

"A successful academy student with quite a bit of practical knowledge about our target."

"My sister would be better for that," Steve said. His two companions looked a little surprised. "I'm not trying to decline. She was just always closer to him."

"Which is why it would be very hard to get her to come along," Sunderland said, leaning forward. His voice dropped a little deeper as he looked straight at Steve. "We're bringing him back for trial, Steve. If he comes willingly or if we carry him out unconscious. It might get ugly."

"That's where I can help."

"Right. You can get us close enough so that we can do this without a scene or collateral damage."

"Tell me about Euphrates."

"It was a Separatist storehouse, so it's pretty much not a place we're welcome. All we really need to know is that it's a dingy little hovel pretty far from main trade lines. Mainly agricultural, with one tiny city right near the only functional landing station worth noting."

"This ship is going to set off all his alarms, then."

"Noted, but I'm glad to see you think of these things," Sunderland said. He smiled when he said it, but Steve had a hard time mirroring the look. Sunderland was pedantic. He might have graduated a year ago, but he talked like he thought he was an admiral.

"We're meeting up with a merchant vessel already in orbit. It's a Security front so we can travel unnoticed. We'll use one of their landing shuttles to get down to the city."

"Is he alone?"

"What question are you really asking, Steve?" Sunderland said, with the patient tones of a therapist. Steve considered not answering.

"You want me to divulge that I have some secret fantasy he isn't aligned with separatist remnants, Ensign," he sighed. "Whereas what I meant is will we need to retrieve him from inside a circle of allies or is he on his own in this backwater slum?"

Morris smiled a little. Steve felt a little pride that the enlisted man reacted to his anger. Sunderland nodded, again like an objective therapist. "We don't have precise information, as our people on the ground are very much not in the loop. We haven't told them what to look for on the chance they might spook him. It appears he is alone, though. There haven't been any meetings with others on any regular basis nor any activity that indicates involvement with an ongoing plot."

"What is he doing?"

"According to our sources," Sunderland said, opening up a folded piece of paper in his pocket. "He's been buying a lot of food and scavenging electronics from junk dealers."

"Do the analysts know what it means?"

"The food indicates he's planning to go into hiding. Maybe offworld, maybe going hermit into the wilds. The electronics they can't figure out. He never demonstrated your skill with devices or had any special training at the academy that would relate to antique machines. But everything he's buying is at least 20 years old."

"I honestly don't know either," Steve admitted. "All I can say is that it tells me we need to move fast."

"That was our take as well," Sunderland indicated, shaking the piece of paper. "In fact, that's about all Command had to say on the topic. We're going to need your brain a lot on this, and maybe you'll even be in the action. You ready for it?"

Steve looked down at the black jacket and black pants. He didn't have the boots on yet, if they could even find any in his size, but it didn't really matter. He was finally in action. Like he would have been years ago if his brother hadn't screwed things up and made them implement a minimum age at the academy. "I've been waiting a lifetime to do something useful, Sir."

"That's what I like to hear," Sunderland smiled as he stood, then saluted. "Morris, finish getting him decked out and we'll do an all hands in an hour."

"Yes, sir," Morris saluted lazily from the floor. Sunderland shook his head in mock exasperation and headed out the door to the main cabin. Steve just watched the somewhat hazy reflection of the tall, dark man in a black uniform staring back from the cupboard door. Morris was smiling as he buttoned up his own uniform jacket and checked the loads in his weapons.

Chapter 18

Anna sat in the dark, watching out the little window. Stars blinked past at high speed. She knew it was an optical illusion. The ship hadn't had time to build much speed after launching. It still felt amazing to be in space.

She pulled her robe tighter, then started moving. It was slow going in the dark, because the hold was full of boxes. She shuffled at first, bumping her shins, and then found the main corridor. She ran her hands along the boxes as she moved. They were all different shapes and sizes. Some sat alone on the floor. Others were piled high on the walls.

Anna walked as far as she could, feeling her way, then realized it was finally a wall in front of her and not another row of boxes. The generic Fleet power switches had never made her so happy before, as she ran her fingers along the raised plastic rectangle. She'd never thought of them before, but now she knew why it was good to have something any crewman could find by touch.

The lights came on low. Normally, Anna figured, that little light would have meant nothing. Coming from the dark she'd been in since launch, it was clearer than daylight. Yet another invention of some clever man like her father, building ships that did exactly what was needed by the crew.

The room was a mess. It looked like it'd been half-emptied and the remainder thrown all over trying to find something that was missing.

She moved quickly among the boxes. Canned fruit and beans. Toilet tissue. All sorts of generic supplies needed by the academy and the outposts around it.

Including a series of crates marked "uniforms."

Anna pried at the top with her hands and it was sealed. She mumbled to herself at her luck, before seeing the large screwdriver sticking out of the seams on another box a few stacks away.

The only shirts were men's shirts without logo or design, looking like the work shirts the enlisted men doing labor jobs would wear. Even the smallest one felt too big, as she pulled it on and kept digging for anything else.

The uniform pants, though, were perfect. Not the heavy material of a tactical suit, which all the cadets dreamed of wearing, but the loose cargo pants of a shipboard officer. It wasn't a proper uniform, but it felt great to find real clothes.

Even better was the underwear. "I know mom said to always wash it first," she told herself, changing out of her pajamas in the shadow of the box lid. "But this is an emergency."

Anna wished for a mirror as she buttoned the shirt and tied the bottom off in a bunch around her waist. Not anything that would pass inspection, she was sure, but it was clean and actual clothing. After crawling around in torn pajamas for an hour, it was pleasant.

"Fan out!" she heard someone yelling, just as the door started to click. Anna dove into the clothing crate, pulling the lid down behind her. It didn't seal, but she hoped it wasn't obvious.

"Go! Go!" a woman's voice yelled. Anna heard footsteps running all throughout the room. She tried to count their numbers, but the echoes from the room and from the crate were just too much.

"Lights were on," she heard someone calling. "No signs of activity yet."

She waited, listening to the noises. The crate was bigger than her bed back home. Maybe even bigger than the car her father insisted on polishing and waxing every weekend. There was no question she'd be visible if they looked, though.

Anna tried to move some of the uniform parts out of the way, to make a hiding hole. The plastic rustled as she pushed, so she stopped. She held her breath, her heart beating in her ears, waiting. No one seemed to have noticed, judging by the running steps and the noises.

She settled in, carefully, trying not to move anything. The plastic moved a little, but the layer of pants was fairly comfortable. Anna closed her eyes, exhaling with relief.

Then the top of the crate came flying open.

Four gun barrels pointed in.

A tall dark-skinned woman held Anna's pajamas in her hand. "You forgot something."

Anna raised her hands and sat up slowly. The rifles were military issue. The four women watching her didn't look it. Only the black woman holding the pajamas had a short cut. One other had a bob sort of like Anna's. The other two had long and spiky looks that made her uncomfortable. One looked a little offended, Anna saw, seeing the face glaring at her. The other just smiled, pointing her rifle a little higher.

"I didn't mean to come aboard. I was trying to get out of the way back in the hangar."

"All of that gunfire? You know what was going on?" The woman with the short hair spoke. The rest of them just waited.

"No. I was, umm, with my boyfriend there. Just hanging out, you know? He ran for the elevators and I got lost in the dark."

"Typical," the short-haired woman said, but the black woman gave her a look that was very clear. "Shut up" was plain to see.

"Don't they have a curfew? And isn't this a little underdressed for hanging out?"

"Are you my mother?" Anna asked. She tried to make it sound like Melina would have said it. Remembering the classmate left behind in the gunfire made her icy look waver.

"Nice attitude, kid," the leader of the group said. She pointed down and all of the rifles relaxed. "This is a supplies transport. We don't veer from our course for any reason. You're stuck onboard for now."

"Maybe I can help out?"

"If you're sucking up to avoid stowaway charges, forget it. I don't care enough to file charges. You might be in AWOL trouble, though, as we maintain radio silence between stops."

"What's your next stop?"

"A tiny little two-guard listening post near Mars. Then back to Earth to refuel and take on supplies. Then two months of repeating the same loop."

"Not the fancy life of a Fleet pilot, is it?" one of the spiky haired women asked. Anna was surprised by the calm and cultured voice. Underneath the wild hair and makeup, the face reminded her of someone. Some movie actor, maybe, because the cheekbones and eyes were both model-quality.

"I'd like to help out, if I can. Just to...stay busy, I guess."

"And not go back to whoever was shooting at you?

"I don't know what you mean."

The captain smiled. "Of course not. Keep the clothes. We'll just write them off as ruined in transport. But get out of that crate and come along. We were playing cards before you interrupted us."

One of the spiky woman held out a strong arm and helped Anna over the edge. She landed carefully in her sock feet, careful of the cluttered floor, and saw the captain was watching her move. She didn't say anything, but Anna saw a little smile she didn't understand. It made the butterflies dance in her stomach again.

Chapter 19

Steve waited at the back of the little knot of people, watching Sunderland and Mayberry talk with the captain of the merchant vessel. With the short hair and straight back, there was no question the merchant had been military and still looked the part. The way his crew hung around, weapons ready, made Steve uncomfortable. Morris just leaned on a crate and watched it all, so Steve tried to do the same.

"These guys don't care about our security clearances," Morris whispered. "This is real spy stuff here on the frontier."

Steve looked at the crew again. There were eight of them, wearing civilian shipsuits of all different cuts and styles. All of them were men and all looked to be fairly large and muscular.

"They look like more of an assault force than our team."

"Because looks aren't everything," Morris responded. After a moment, looking over the men that studied them carefully, he turned back. "Although I'm sure they've had their hands in things we aren't supposed to know about."

"That's a deal," the merchant captain said suddenly, ending the quiet conversation that had been only between the two men. His crew visibly relaxed and Steve felt his legs shiver underneath as all the tension released. The captain reached into the pocket of his cargo pants and pulled out a stack of ID cards, which he flipped through like a poker dealer. He pulled one out and flashed it, showing the official identification of a Asian-looking Fleet officer. "This will work the little black shuttle out back."

Sunderland looked a little offended, but Mayberry smiled and gave him a push as he took the card. "That's stolen property," Sunderland said as they cleared the circle of armed watchers and reached Morris.

"Right. Tell Security. Oh, wait," Morris mocked. "We're on the frontier and there is no Security. And everyone here already works for Security. So...not so stolen."

"Richard's right, Allan," Mayberry said, holding up the ID card. "It's a fake made to look like a stolen key card. The security numbers don't match up to the ones they were using when this was supposedly issued. They are too new."

"That's a sad man that would know that sort of trivia," Morris added.

"Or an effective investigator when Security promotes us all," Mayberry smiled back. "Are we ready?"

The team nodded. Even Airman Lao, who didn't say much and hung back further than the others. "Here's the plan," Mayberry said. "We take the shuttle to the main landing pad. We make contact with a local source. We get Trilouis into custody as soon as we pinpoint a location. Then we get back here, pick up our ship, and get back to Earth in a day."

"What if we don't pinpoint him that quickly?" Sunderland asked.

"Then we withdraw and get out ship and come back in force. We have surprise today, but it won't last."

"Makes sense," Steve added and everyone nodded.

"Ok. Check your gear and get back here in five. We board the shuttle as soon as we're here. We're launching in fifteen, whether you're belted in or not," Mayberry said.

Steve turned, then waited for Morris to catch up. The way the merchant crew was watching him made him a lot less sure than he felt among Team A.

"Wait a minute," one of the crew called out as Steve turned back to look for Morris. The man was older than Steve first expected. His hair wasn't blond, but grey, and up close his face was carved with deep lines.

"Can I help you?" Morris said, popping up next to Steve and standing with a hand on the butt of his stunner.

"You're Wroclaw's kid, aren't you?" the older man asked.

"Stanis? He's my father," Steve answered.

The older man rolled up a sleeve. On top of his forearm he had a wide tattoo in bright red ink. Steve couldn't make sense of it all, but it looked like a blueprint of part of a ship. "Pacifier-class. I was working for the shipyards when they made them. You were a little kid and used to come with your father."

Steve smiled. "That was a while ago."

"I can see. You're all grown up and out of the academy now. Your dad must be quite proud."

"He is," Morris interrupted before Steve could figure out what to answer. "But we best be going."

"Please do. He won't remember me, but let him know everyone in Engine Cooling Operations very much enjoyed working under him."

"I will. I'm sure he remembers your team," Steve said, as Morris had a hand on his shoulder and was heading him toward the door.

"Odd that someone mentions your dad, isn't it?" Morris asked as they headed through the narrow tunnel back to the AR-14.

"Sort of."

"You close?"

"I grew up with him around quite a bit. I don't see him as much now."

"I wondered where you were," Mayberry said as they came through the tunnel. He stood in the middle of a stack of grey boxes. Lao was picking items from the boxes and stuffing them into four backpacks.

"Old home week for the kid," Morris said. "You made contact with your guy?"

"It's Sunderland's guy. He's from the intelligence side of things," Mayberry answered, hefting one of the packs as Lao zipped it shut.

"I'm waiting until we hit the ground," the other officer answered from the next room, sticking his head back through the door. "I don't want any interception of communication."

"What if he's not home or at the market or something?"

Sunderland rolled his eyes. "With what we pay, people pick up when we call."

"Is your source reliable?" Steve asked. Everything sort of stopped when he said it.

"What do you mean?"

"If he gives us information, is it going to be a hit? Will it be uncorrupted?"

Sunderland sighed, hauling an ammo case back into the room. He resumed loading rounds into empty magazines, which he was stacking into a smaller backpack. "We have expectations of high reliability."

"How is that different from reliable?"

"You're questioning me like you're the commander, not an academy student," Sunderland said. Steve felt the aggression. "I'm the mission commander."

"I'm the one that knows Trilouis. He's of above average intelligence and he has taken more academy courses than anyone his age. He completed the Command and Security training courses, other than graduating."

"That's right. And we graduated," Sunderland added.

"I think the kid's point is that the piece of paper doesn't mean a lot. You're dealing with someone with the same training you have and probably more brains than most of us put together," Morris said. "For all we know, he's assembling an army and has fifty armed men waiting for us. He's been on the run for two years, evading us at every turn."

"We know he doesn't have men. Our sources are more reliable than that. Trilouis has been spotted, usually traveling alone, and not keeping any specific schedule."

"Usually?" Lao asked, pushing a pack toward Morris and strapping one on himself.

"There are several reports which place him in the company of a male child, five or six years old by the watcher's estimate. However they have both been seen separately and it isn't sure if they are associated."

"So we're not the only one bringing a kid to this fight?" Morris laughed. Steve shook his head. He liked it, though. It was like being one of the guys in the locker room after a team practice.

"It's not a fight," Mayberry said. "And we're going to be late for it if we don't get moving."

Chapter 20

"My name is Iris. What's yours?"

Anna looked at the captain, trying to judge what was going on with her. Her face was long and angular, with rounded cheekbones that stuck out and little eyes that were almost hidden under a heavy brow.

"Anna."

"Welcome aboard the ShipCom Industries Transport 103, also know as Flower. It was named after me when I was a little girl, before you start thinking I'm full of myself."

"I'm not sure I'd have made the connection," Anna said, sipping from the mug of hot chocolate they'd given her. It was thick and sweet. They didn't have it at the academy. Empty calories, she'd been told. Wasteful for minds and bodies on a mission. But it tasted great.

"My father captained it before me," the captain said, taking a mug of coffee from a tiny Asian woman with a thick scar across her face, across one eye socket that was covered with a patch. Then she disappeared back into the galley, closing the door, leaving the two of them sitting across a four-person table much like what they had at the academy. "Why are you on my ship, Anna?"

"The hangar was dangerous. I thought I was getting out of the room, but I crawled into your freight elevator."

"Why were you in the hangar?"

"I told you. We were hanging out."

"And someone started shooting?"

"Yes."

"So what about your boyfriend? The one we heard yell?"

"Just a friend. He ran the other way."

"Are you worried for him?" Captain Iris asked. She took a tiny sip from her mug, then held it like she was savoring the taste before taking a quick swallow.

"He's had combat skills," Anna said, as it occurred to her. "He would have been able to get out safely." Or so she could argue.

"So there wasn't a boy?" Iris said after another tiny sip, holding the mug by her face."

"What? Of course there was."

"You're either heartless or not that into him if you aren't worried. You might think academy combat training is the ultimate weapon, but I doubt it. You're smarter than that."

"Go ahead and slag the academy. You probably didn't get in."

Iris didn't react. "I'll save that for later. So if there wasn't a boy, then you probably weren't an innocent bystander. So why the shooting?"

"I don't know. I'm not lying."

Another tiny sip. "Since we won't agree on that, then what do you want us to do about having you aboard? We can't change course and you'll be AWOL as soon as they know you're gone."

Anna grimaced. That would be a big problem. Security might already be searching for her, but her mother would flip. "If I can call out, I can let my family know where I am. They can fix things."

"You got money?"

Anna held up her arms. "I don't even have clothes."

"ShipCom deducts personal calls from our wages. I don't know anyone that's going to volunteer a call back to Earth. That's probably two days pay."

Anna thought. "Well, if I'm here a while I can work it off, right?"

"Doing what? You're what, a first year student?"

"Third. But I can help wherever you need me."

Iris shook her head. "You're lucky we were the ship in port, kid. Some crews hear you say that and you're never seen again."

Anna flushed. "I mean, I can clean or help navigate or whatever."

"Course is locked in. Shanna is on mop duty because she lost at cards. What else?"

Anna felt an uncomfortable itch. "I don't know, Captain."

Iris smiled. "I'm not going to force you to do anything, kid. But you have to realize the academy is a lot safer and cleaner than the real world."

"You say it like you've been there."

"One hundred and tenth out of three hundred in my class, kid. General Operations degree. Ten year veteran before I went private."

Anna was quiet. "I'm sorry for saying those things, then."

"No, you're sorry I called you on it and proved you wrong."

"Yes, I am," she admitted.

The little Asian woman entered and handed a note to the captain, giving a little nod. Anna noticed for the first time that the scar curved around her chin and across the front of her throat. "Lin tells me I have a call waiting. Would you like to come to the bridge?"

"Is that allowed? I mean, the Fleet..."

"This is a commercial vessel, owned by a contractor doing business with the Fleet. They may have strict rules about their bridges. I have one, which is that no one eats at the duty stations."

"I'd love to see it," Anna said. "It's been a while since I've been aboard a moving ship."

Captain Iris nodded, then looked like she might say anything. Anna took too big a drink of her hot chocolate, coughing a little, trying to look busy. Iris nodded again and led the way out of the galley, across the hall to a small silver door. It popped open instantly, revealing an elevator. The captain let her in first, then followed her into the little space and hit a series of buttons.

The rest of the ride was quiet. Anna tried to count floors, to judge the size of the ship, but it was too fast and too quiet to be sure. The captain didn't say anything, but looked at the slip of paper in her hand a few times before folding it and sticking it into her chest pocket as the doors opened.

Anna looked up with some surprise as they exited the small lift. "This looks familiar," she heard herself say, looking around the room.

The front of the room was a giant screen or window. She couldn't tell which at first. The blackness of space could have been right outside the window or projected. The pilot console, right in front of it, had two chairs that were filled by a spiky haired woman and a slim man she hadn't seen before. He looked back over his shoulder as the door entered, nodded, and then went back to checking whatever was on his screen.

"Crew, this is Anna, our stowaway. Anna, this is the crew. You'll have time to meet them over the next couple days and I don't want to deprive you of the adventure."

She nodded and smiled at the two pilots. The only other person in the room was the woman with the bob haircut, sitting at the communications station behind the captain's spot.

"So what is this?" Iris asked, taking a seat at the chair centered behind the pilots. There were an array of buttons and knobs on the arms and sides of the chair. Anna tried to place them all, but too many were replacements or seemingly out of order.

"We have been hailed by two ships that are moving to intercept," the bob said, her hair shaking slightly as she turned to look at the captain. "No identification."

"Did they say anything interesting?"

"Just some angry voices."

Iris turned and looked at Anna for a moment.

"Shira, what's their intercept look like? Can we dodge?"

The spiky haired woman swiveled her chair to look back at the captain. Anna, standing to Iris's side, felt a chill from the way the woman looked at her. "They are coming at two depths, like they are preparing for us to run."

"Then we wait for them and keep on our plotted course. Carlos, can you get a visual?"

The thin little man nodded and flicked a series of switches on the control desk. The screen changed perspective, looking out over the long tail of the ship and the glow of the engines. Two rounded shapes were barely visible against the field of stars.

"I don't know them," the man said after a moment where everyone stared at the shapes.

"Me either," the captain said. "Kid?"

"What?"

"You're the brainy academy type. Identify them."

Anna stared at the screen a moment. "Hull shape is consistent with the old Miami-class shuttles often used by Titan freebooters."

"We're a little far from Titan," the captain said.

"Well, that's what they look like. I can't tell you where they are from."

"Accents weren't Titan, either," the woman with the bob added. "Clipped and generic."

"Bossy rude pricks with bland accents? Where have I heard that?" the captain said. The spiky haired woman and the male pilot laughed. "That was an academy joke, kid," she said after a moment, making them laugh again.

"I figured."

"They always do have the smart ones," Iris said.

"They are hailing again. AV signal this time, not just audio."

"Light it up," Iris said, leaning back in her chair.

The screen flickered and half of it resolved into a tall man in a uniform Anna didn't recognize. It was black like a tactical suit, but with silver strips on the chest and shoulders that looked reflective.

"Come to a full stop, merchant captain," the man said. Iris looked at her and she looked away. The voice was really pompous and had the sort of bland accent taught as "proper" by the academy staff, to improve Fleet communication.

"Good day to you, Sir. Who are you and why should I be stopping?"

"I'm afraid the answers to those questions are classified. We'll have permission from ShipCom to board their ship in about two minutes. I wanted to save you the trouble of our ships using gravitizers to halt you."

"So either I stop or you drag me to a halt, probably carving half the shielding off my hull in the process? Where's the part where you introduce yourselves and ask nicely?"

The man smiled. "Captain!" the pilot yelled, before the entire ship rocked. Anna grabbed onto the back of the Captain's chair. Iris braced herself with giant hands on the sides of the chair. The pilots yanked their harnesses into place. The communications woman laughed as she fell out of her chair, giggling as she lay on the ground next to it.

"That was one round from one of our guns. We could take you apart in an instant."

"Still doesn't tell me why you don't just ask nicely," Iris said, leaning forward.

"We don't have to ask, Captain. You have someone on board that is coming with us. The only question is whether you're alive when we leave."

"And who is this you're looking for?"

"Don't be coy, Captain. I can see her standing next to you."

"Why the kid?"

"Because."

Iris turned to the communications station, where the woman had righted herself back into the chair. "Cut it," she said, quietly. The screen went back to the view of the two ships, now much closer, over the tail of the Flower.

"Not a chatty group," Iris said. She punched the intercom button on her chair arm. "Hernandez, get Mei Lin to look at a picture of those ships and see what she says."

"Give me a minute," the voice crackled back over the speaker.

"So, kid. Got anything else you want to tell me? Boyfriend the jealous type, maybe?"

"Those are Miami-class ships. That's all I know."

"Captain," the voice called out of the speaker on the chair. "Mei Lin says they are Miami-class ships. I showed her the still photo of the caller and she tells me they are Dragoons."

"Dragons?"

"Two 'o', Captain. I asked her that myself."

"If she thinks we're questioning her spelling, we'll be on oatmeal for a week," the captain said. Hernandez laughed a little and then the crackle of the speaker went quiet. "Always keep things light, kid. Your crew appreciates it."

"I know what Dragoons are," Anna said.

"I do too. So why don't you tell me and I'll tell you if you're right?"

"Internal security forces."

"Too short for full credit, but close enough. The Fleet's secret police, keeping their messes out of the public eye."

"I think mine was less biased of an answer."

"Ask Mei Lin sometime, kid," Iris said. "What's the status of our two guests?"

"Three. A third just joined them. They are holding a steady distance."

"They haven't turned us to swiss cheese yet. Any guesses?"

"They want their target alive."

"Also not good enough for full credit."

"They want me alive."

"Correct, Anna. Why are they after you?"

"To take me back to the academy, I guess," she answered.

"They'd send Security for that."

"Not if they are scrambling all forces."

"Sure, but why would they do that? One kid walking away isn't anything new."

"I don't know," Anna said, but she saw the captain's look. She didn't buy it.

"The second ship is hailing us."

"On screen, then," the captain said.

The uniform was the same, but this man was slighter with a giant beard and a mountain of hair piled on his head. Anna thought one of his eyes was blocked by a reflection at first. Then she realized the little red light was his eye. She felt a little shiver. Putting robotic enhancements in a human had been illegal in Fleet space for a very long time.

"Captain Iris Belmonte. It is a pleasure."

"Commander Ben Luis. I had heard you were in prison."

"We'll catch up another time, lovely. Unfortunately you have some contraband onboard and you know what happens then."

"We get boarded and searched?"

"So you do remember."

"If you set foot aboard this ship, it will be the last step you ever take," the captain said. Anna looked in surprise. She hadn't raised her voice or changed her tone.

"So my little Asian flower is still working for you, is she?"

"I meant I'd do it myself, Luis."

"If you just turn over the girl, there is no need for anyone to be unpleasant."

"First, I'm not sure any teenage girl should be unsupervised aboard your ship. I've seen those thugs in shiny uniforms you call a crew."

"Slander, Captain. Merchant types always do resent the Fleet, even us mere auxiliary forces."

Anna felt the shiver again. It wasn't just the tone to his voice, which was greasy and smarmy. She'd thought the same things. This ship wasn't as organized as the Fleet and the crew looked funny, so it must not be as good. The warped mirror of the Fleet she was looking at in the viewscreen made her ill.

"Second, tell me why you want her," the captain said.

"She is absent without leave from the academy."

"You're doing truant duty now?"

"I don't ask questions, Belmonte. Maybe you'd still be in a real uniform if you tried that."

"Selling me on blindly obeying isn't going to get you too far, Luis."

"Commander Luis, merchant captain. There's a vast distinction there you'd do well to remember."

"Like that computer in your head remembers everything?" she said, in that same tone. Anna almost laughed as the man on the screen visibly reddened and a vein popped out over his eye.

Then the ship shook. Anna grabbed the back of the chair and the rest of the crew looked at the helm.

Luis laughed. "That would be Major Andrews and his boarding party approaching in the dead spot on your sensors. You've got about a minute to surrender the fugitive before we take your ship by force."

"Cut comm.," the captain said. The screen went dark. "All crew," she said, hitting the speaker buttons on the side of her chair, "prepare to be boarded. Lock in. Plan Viva. Repeat, Viva."

Anna looked up as the fans stopped moving. It was the sound cadets were drilled to recognize from the first moments aboard a ship or station in space.

"The circulators," Anna started, but the captain nodded.

"We're sealing ourselves in important areas and opening the rest of the ship to vacuum. If they plan to board, they better have brought their spacesuits."

Chapter 21

Sephalos scratched. The rest of the men in the shuttle laughed. He looked up to see them all looking at him, from all around the small cabin.

"There aren't really shorts for the outfit," Morris laughed. The rest of the team laughed even more openly. "Especially wool ones. Really rough wool ones."

"That's rude," Steve said, laughing with them.

"It's a rite of passage," Mayberry said from the pilot's chair. "Welcome to the team."

Steve beamed. "Really?"

"We all went through it."

"Speak for yourself," Sunderland said from the other chair up front.

"All of us not dorky enough to read the tech manuals and know full outfit specs prior to deployment," Morris said. Everyone laughed, including Sunderland.

"Good point, Richard," Sunderland said. "Now everyone buckle in and try not to scratch. We're setting down in a minute."

Steve felt the butterflies. His whole stomach shook as the rockets fired and the shuttle started slowing. He felt lunch bouncing around in his stomach and tried hard to swallow.

"You ok?" Morris asked from the bench across the way. He was wearing a black tactical suit and had his helmet at the ready. He also had three pistols in holsters, two on his belt and one of his shoulder. He looked like a recruiting poster.

"First trip," Steve breathed. Talking helped.

"So this will be your first new planet?"

"Yes. I've been on ships and stations, but never another planet."

"If I'd known, we'd have hazed you on that too."

Everyone laughed, until the ship rocked. "Atmosphere," Mayberry said.

"Either that or you're a worse pilot than I heard," Sunderland quipped.

"Landing beacons are in sight. Get ready. Steve, you and Sunderland are the first ones out."

"The kid?" Morris asked. "Sorry," he said when he saw Steve's hurt look.

"Throw a poncho over your suit," Sunderland said, turning from the navigator's station to look into the cabin. He tossed a little bundle and Steve snapped it out of the air. "It isn't a great disguise, but it will work for us."

"Just a sailor and an apprentice from some commercial rig?"

"You got it, kid. You're smarter than Morris already."

"In three. Two. Down," Mayberry said, but it was pretty obvious. The ship shook and rocked, then Steve felt his stomach jump as they came to a stop.

"Door open," Sunderland said, punching buttons. By the time the back of the ship cranked open, Morris and Lao had their helmets on and guns ready. They knelt by the door, behind bulkheads, covering the exit. "We're up."

Steve followed a step behind, tugging the rough cloth over his head. It was scratchy fabric that smelled like oil. The sort of thing an apprentice would wear. Sunderland had thrown on a cleaner version of the same.

Sunderland waited right off the little ramp leading to the ground. Steve followed, feeling the odd bounce of a different gravity. Off the ship, the sun was high in the sky and the air warmer than Steve expected. It was hard to breathe the wet air as he bounced down the ramp.

"You ready?"

Steve nodded. "Where is our contact?"

"Right here," a little voice answered.

Steve looked down in surprise. Sunderland took a step back, his hand dropping to his side.

Beside a fuel barrel, almost hidden by shadows, was a little boy. Maybe five or six, Steve guessed, with a lot of shaggy blond hair and a dirty face. His eyes glowed bright in the noontime sun.

"Red dwarf," Sunderland said.

"Black hole," the kid answered. The way he talked made Steve think he was bored.

"What's the news?"

"About a half klick away," the little boy replied. He pointed into the distance. "Red house, in an empty lot."

"Get lost," Sunderland said, tossing a credit stick at the kid. He snagged it from the air with a hand that moved too fast for Steve to follow. Steve looked at Sunderland in surprise, but the soldier was already looking back up the ramp. "Let's go, team."

The other three men marched out. They had their helmets in place. Lao handed one to Steve as Mayberry gave Sunderland his. Mayberry also carried a long rifle that he handed off. "Go!" Mayberry yelled and they started to run. Steve took off a second later, watching the men run in front of him.

Chapter 22

Anna looked at the vent, waiting for something to happen. It stayed quiet and still.

"Relax, Anna," the captain said. "We have five hours of air in the bridge and auxiliary tanks in reserve. Even if they come with suits," she said, but she looked up in surprise as alarms buzzed.

"On visual," the helmsman said, hitting a series of buttons.

There were six men. They had spacesuits and the captain swore, some words Anna wasn't sure she'd heard before, and she'd grown up around Fleet people. All of them were carrying long guns.

"Those aren't stunners," the captain said after a moment of watching.

"They are pretty new," Shira said. "Nothing I used."

"RivTech 8903," Anna answered. "Rubber-based projectiles that will go through a body but not a hull."

"Hernandez," the captain said, hitting the chair's switches, "what can you see?"

The voice came back even more crackly than before. "Six. Armed. Moving slow, but they know the layout, I'd say."

"How long before you can get to the bridge?"

There was a long pause. "Another two minutes," Hernandez answered.

"Keep going. We'll need your defense."

"Understood," the woman answered in a burst of static and crackles.

"Captain," the helmsman said after a moment of watching the advancing boarding party. "I'm pretty sure they aren't heading here."

"Why?" Iris asked, walking up to where the man sat. Anna followed.

"Fastest route here would have been to cut past engineering and access the lift shaft or emergency stairs. They turned before then and are cutting close to the galley," Carlos said.

Iris swore again, pretty much every word Anna had heard. Her step back to her chair was more of a jump that reminded Anna of Zero G exercises. "Hernandez, how far out are you?"

"They are watching their six pretty closely, so slower than planned. Another two minutes."

"Double time. They are heading toward the galley."

The ship shook again. Anna looked up at the screen. One small explosion had already pitted the door to the galley. A spacesuited soldier was pinning another box of wires to the door.

"If they blow it open, they'll depressurize..." Anna started to

147

say, but the captain nodded.

"Luis has been a pain for a long time, but I didn't think he'd use this as a cover for revenge."

"Can you repressurize the ship? Before they open it?"

The captain shook her head. Anna looked around to see the rest of the crew staring at their control pads. "We need to wait on Hernandez."

"She's on her way to the bridge, right? To help us?"

"Not our bridge," Iris said, with a wry smile. "But that doesn't help us much at the moment."

"We do have emergency suits here on the bridge," the spiky-haired woman at navigation said.

"Emergency. We're not there yet," Iris said.

"If they blow that door, we are," the man added. "Captain," he finished, after a moment.

"Let's see what we have," the captain said. The man stood, and for the first time Anna saw he was missing a leg. He didn't have a replacement like some of the veterans she'd met at the Fleet, talking about their experiences. He had a crutch that looked to be carved from wood. In a couple of steps he was at the wall and clicking open one of the drawers. He reached in and pulled out two plastic packages. "Medium and small. Only two," he said. "Apparently we restocked poorly after the Nirvana incident."

Anna tried to remember anything by that name. She'd heard about an anti-pirate mission from her mom, a year or so ago, but couldn't remember anything involving merchant ships.

"I'm not going to fit a medium," Iris said, swearing some more for punctuation. "No one here will."

"I could," Anna said. They all looked at her. She felt the nerves but stood straight. "We need to get the small one to the galley, right? I can wear one and take the other."

"You can't do this," Iris said. "Too risky, even if they weren't looking for you."

"She is the only one that fits," the communications officer said. "She's got the same build as Hernandez and we bought that size for her."

Iris was quiet a moment, staring at Anna in a way that was uncomfortable. "Ok," she said. "Chris, get the specs on screen."

The spiky woman nodded and the screen changed from the six soldiers to a map of the ship. "This is the bridge," the captain pointed to the larger square. Anna recognized it instantly. These are service tunnels that run alongside the air lines," indicating narrower boxes running the length of the ship. "Insert here, crawl a hundred meters, take a left, then another ten, and you're over the galley."

"That's a long crawl in a few minutes," Chris said from the helm.

"How many minutes?" Anna asked. The screen changed again, to where they were now wiring a third box to the door.

"Maybe two until they get the door open. Mei Lin will have set up a barricade that probably buys you another two."

Anna's eyes grew big. "I better get moving," she said. She took the package from the man, shaking the plastic suit out of its bag. The oxygen cylinder on the back was fully charged, according to the gauge, but she took a test breath anyway. The captain nodded in approval.

"A little tight on the shoulders, but good," the captain said, helping her pull the snug suit over her clothes. "It's not as fragile as it feels, but avoid anything really sharp."

"Or bullets," Chris said from the helm, earning a look from the captain. Anna nodded, because it was good advice.

"You're a brave kid, cadet, but don't go thinking you're a superhero because you go to the fancy school."

"I wouldn't," Anna started.

"Of course you do. Cadets are taught from day one that they are the smartest and best and the saviors of mankind. Just remember, those enlisted dropouts in the hallway have guns that kill."

Anna nodded. She wasn't like that. She knew it. But there was no question it was scary and dangerous. "Open the grate. I best get moving."

Chapter 23

Anna crawled as fast as she could. The suit helped her slide faster, but the lack of wear on her knees also meant that getting traction was hard. She felt sweat on her face, hidden behind a mask so that she couldn't reach it, a few seconds into her scramble.

The tunnel was dark. The only light came from vents into the other rooms, most of which were dark. Power had been cut to them along with the air circulation.

It reminded her of an exercise during her first year. They'd had to crawl through vents and tunnels aboard a ship in the bay. There hadn't been suits. There certainly hadn't been anyone with guns. All of the students had been thrilled to even be aboard a Fleet ship and no one had given much thought to the "why" of it all.

Anna reached the bend. She looked up in surprise at the flat grey wall before her. It had gone much faster than she'd thought. She wished she could wipe the sweat away, but in a moment she'd entered the sealed galley and could breathe.

The ship tipped. Anna grabbed for the wall, not finding anything to hold. She slid on her side, until she thumped against what had been the ceiling.

"All crew, battlestations," the captain's voice said in her ear. "Kid, bridge," she added briefly a moment later.

"Almost there, captain."

"Get back here, cadet," she barked.

Anna twisted back onto her knees and looked. She couldn't see past the bend and all around her was just grey metal. All the way back was the order. It was also not accomplishing her mission. Anna kept moving forward.

Two more dark vents, over store rooms, and then the light of the galley. The seal was a plastic cover, so she could still see. It was like she remembered from before. A few tables and soft yellow walls.

There was a rush of air escaping as she triggered the lock and waited a moment, for the slats to slide open, then she levered her legs into the gap and jumped just as the safety system resealed the breach.

The fall was longer than she thought. She tried to duck and roll, but caught an ankle. The pain shot up her leg and she rolled, cracking her shoulder against on of the tables as she stopped.

The door was open. There was a safety seal over it, but the metal was gone. She scrambled, waiting for gunfire, ducking under the table. It was just quiet.

"Cadet, can you hear me?"

"Yes, ma'am," Anna responded.

"You're in so much trouble I don't know where to start. Get back up into that tunnel now."

"The door," she started, but then something caught her eye.

"We know, cadet. Now get out of there."

Anna stood. She wasn't sure what she was seeing. Then the bile was at the back of her throat. She clawed as her face mask, getting it off just as the vomit splashed onto the table in front of her.

It was a body. A torso, really. No arms or legs, just stumps that were raw red meat, leaking fluids onto the floor. The head was gone, as far as she could tell, but she didn't move. She couldn't move.

"Captain," she breathed into the microphone, still by her face and now soggy and smelling.

"Tunnel, kid," she said.

"There's a body," she started.

"Tunnel."

Anna turned and looked up at the ceiling. If she piled a couple of chairs, she could reach it. She grabbed one and put it in place, then turned for another. There was a body under the table. She choked back the scream and the remains of her lunch, her stomach doing everything to empty. This one was all in one piece, but his chest was blown open. The Dragoon uniform was a mess of ripped fabric mixed with red pulp and little white pieces of bone.

"Captain, I...," Anna started.

"It is o. k. if she waits," a computerized voice broke onto the line.

"You all right, Lin?" Iris asked.

"I am unhurt," she said. "Come back to my office, cadet."

Anna moved slowly, afraid of every corner of the room. She slid into the cooking area and almost screamed again. Three more men were on the floor. They were dead, with blank eyes staring forever at the ceiling. Beyond them was a little desk with a tablet and monitor, where the little Asian woman sat.

Next to her was an oxygen tank with a makeshift facemask made from kitchen supplies. There was some sort of tube and a plastic bag on the end for her face. Next to that were two large knives, their blades chipped and covered in blood. Lin's hands were also bloody and there was a large stain across the front of her grey apron.

"It is not my blood. Do not worry," the voice said in Anna's ear.

"I don't think that's what worries her, Lin. Or me. Report," the captain's voice called out.

The small woman smiled as she typed quickly on the pad's keyboard. As she did it, the computerized voice spoke over the radio. "Five dead. One made a break back toward his ship. Wounded, but I did not pursue."

"Hernandez, report," the captain said.

"A couple seconds, Captain," she said. Everyone waited, then the ship shook again. "We're free."

"Get inside, fast," Iris said. "Lin, have the cadet help you. Space those bodies."

"Captain, I am not sure she is well," Lin typed.

"She's well enough to disobey my order to get out of there. So she can help clean up the mess."

"Understood," Mei Lin typed, looking up at Anna while she did it. There was a little smile on the corner's of her mouth. When she stood, Anna noticed there was a glob of red pulp stuck in her hair, just above her left ear. This time the dry heaves came with a black flash that put her on the ground.

Chapter 24

The house was where they heard it would be. The rest of the city block was gone. There were a few boards and beams in a couple of lots, but mainly it was thin, dry grass and black crusty dirt. Trash dotted the entire landscape, blowing in the wind and piling around the longest grass. The doors of the house were wide open and a man walked in and out of the house a couple of times as they crouched behind the nearest cover. The rusted out hulk of an old commercial transport smelled of fuel oil and dirt, making Steve's nose itch.

"Can you identify him?" Sunderland's voice was low and heavy. He fingered the trigger guard of his weapon as he stared.

Steve shook his head. "Not at this distance. The height and weight are what I remember. Do you have binoculars?"

"On the ship," Mayberry growled, pawing through the little kit on his belt.

"I can't make a clear call," Steve said.

"We go in," Sunderland said. "Lao, Morris take point. The rest of us will be right behind you."

The two soldiers crouched, looking over the deserted area. They waited until the man stepped back into the house. Then they ran, keeping low, stopping only when they reached the sides of the red house. Steve took off right behind Sunderland and Mayberry, keeping as low as he could and trying to follow their path out of sight of the house windows.

Steve watched the others get closer to the door as he closed in. "Go!" Sunderland barked just as Steve dove into the shade of the house.

Lao and Morris rushed the open door, Morris entering first and spinning left as Lao went the other way. Steve followed as the officers entered, his hand on the weapon in his belt. His heart was racing. He felt like he might get sick.

"Is it him?" Morris barked. Steve rushed forward. The man on the ground had a thick beard and his hair was shaggy. The height was the same, but up close he was too thin and haggard.

"I don't think so."

"I need more than that," Morris growled. The man on the ground looked up but didn't say anything. He wasn't struggling, but just letting them hold him.

"Let me look," Steve said, getting down.

"Be careful," Mayberry warned.

The man looked in confusion as Steve looked into his eyes. Steve reached out and pushed the hair back, then poked the beard. "Not him," Steve said.

"Get out of here. Back to the ship," Mayberry barked. Steve turned, just as the little boy stepped into the room.

"Freeze!" Morris barked. All the guns turned. The kid raised his hands.

"Stupid coming here after giving us bad info," Sunderland said.

"Stupid listening to someone after only the first countersign because he looks harmless," the blond boy said. Except he didn't look at Sunderland or the others. Steve felt a chill as the boy stared right at him, despite all of the other men and their guns.

"Really, Sunderland?" Morris asked. "That's not procedure."

"He's five, Rick. Or looks five."

"I'm eight," the kid said. "And I know who you are."

"And we'll know you as soon as we run your visual through the system. You'll be in a protective unit your grandkids can shave."

"Logically impossible I'd have grandkids if I was in lockup, isn't it?" the kid asked and Steve felt like he was listening to himself. It was as annoying as people told him.

"Get on the ground," Morris said.

"I have a message for you," the kid said.

"On the ground!"

"Mr. Trilouis didn't know you were coming. He's here, but won't be for long once I get some things I need off your ship."

"Down!" Morris said, grabbing the kid. Except the little boy wasn't standing in place anymore and Morris only caught him a glancing blow on the chest. The kid somersaulted backwards and was back on his feet before Morris finished the push.

"I was just going to make clear that this wasn't his doing and you shouldn't hold it against him. His crimes are political."

"Down!" Morris barked again, as he and Lao advanced. The kid smiled, and then everything went black. Steve felt his stomach twist like he was on a roller coaster or riding with a bad pilot. Everything smelled like dirt and mold and he started sneezing.

"Lights!" Sunderland barked. A second later, two lamps light and then a third. Steve took a moment longer, digging into his pocket of supplies until the light turned up. He looped the net over his head and turned it on, like an old miner's lamp.

It was fitting. All around was grey rock, streaked with black streaks of minerals. Steve watched Lao and Morris move, scouting the area.

"What happened? Where are we?" Steve asked. No one answered. Steve looked around. Grey walls, streaked with lines of lighter rock. The floor held footprints, much to Steve's relief. Other people had been here.

"There's a tunnel this way," Lao's quiet voice split the silence.

"Here too," Morris said. "And a third."

"Are we getting a signal from the ship?" Sunderland asked. Mayberry was already tapping on the miniature tablet he had on a wrist strap.

"It's weak. Too weak to give us an exact position, but it can head us back into the light. However far that might be."

"Then we start marching."

"Where are we heading?" Steve asked as they started walking.

It was quiet a moment before Sunderland answered. Steve started to wonder if they were ignoring him. "We're going to find that kid and figure out what he did to us. Then we're going to find Trilouis, who I know is behind this. Then we're going to do the job we came to do," Sunderland growled.

"I can answer part of that," Steve said after a few more feet walking up the rocky path. It was wide enough for a fleet of trucks to pass through, which made Steve pretty sure where they were.

"That Trilouis is behind it? I knew that. Even Lao knew that," Morris joked. No one really laughed. The trail was getting steep.

"We're in the tunnels that the original colony ships dug when they burrowed in on landing. Probably about two miles from the spaceport."

Mayberry looked at the tablet. "Could be. Too much rock to get a good signal."

"How do you know this, kid?" Morris asked, turning back to look. His feet kept stepping over rocks and pebbles in a way that amazed Steve, who could barely stop staring at his own feet.

"Standard design. I've seen a lot of documentary footage. My dad worked on some of the original ships. It was big with me when I was little."

"Because you're big now?" Morris joked with big dramatic eyes, then saw Steve's face crash. "Just kidding, Cadet."

"No problem. My fault. But yeah, standard tunnels."

"So how did we get here?"

"The reason they really want Trilouis back so badly," Steve said. Morris and Sunderland shared a look and then both looked at Mayberry. The three then looked at Steve with anxious expressions. "Don't pretend."

Sunderland looked at Mayberry again, and then Sunderland looked at Morris and they all exchanged looks. Steve felt his smile fade as they shook their heads at each other and turned back to him. "We want to recover a fugitive because we were ordered to do so," Mayberry said.

"You weren't told to recover anything else? A box about so big?" Steve asked, making the shape with his hand. It wasn't much larger than his head, rectangular with a number of holes on it he tried to pantomime. "About a foot long, half that as thick, with holes of about a half inch across all over the top?"

"Never heard of it, kid," Morris answered. They had all stopped walking and were gathered around him.

"Oh," Steve said. He looked up at all of them, clearly thinking.

"What is it?" Mayberry asked. He was anxious. Steve couldn't tell if they were faking or not.

"One of the three telephase generators built by the Fleet. The greatest weapon ever devised and he stole it and ran. You sure you never heard of it?"

Chapter 25

Anna sat in one of the chairs off to the side of the bridge. As long as she watched her feet, in borrowed slippers since her shoes were ruined with blood, the room didn't spin.

"Any better?" the captain asked, walking between stations. Anna looked up, saw three of her and shook her head. The shaking only made it worse.

"Sorry, captain," Anna said with her hand over her mouth.

"Kid, you saw one of the more gruesome sights I could imagine," Iris said. Anna grabbed her stomach, and then her head, as the images flashed back. "That'd mess up hardened combat veterans. Just rest for a few."

Anna nodded, slowly and tried to smile. The captain returned it, but it faded as she turned back to the bridge. The rest of the crew had arrived, assembling in one place for the first time since Anna had stowed away.

"Ok, crew," the captain said. Anna listened, but her eyes were focused on the black and white slippers rocking back and forth. The diamond pattern, alternating black and white, kept shifting to her eyes as her feet moved. "Luis is still out there. He's seen the other Dragoon ship drift away and he has to know they've been incapacitated."

The images flashed back into Anna's mind. Her stomach didn't heave so much this time.

"I'm sure we can outrun him," the helmsman said. He was turned in his chair, his little stump of a leg resting on the arm of the chair.

"No doubt. But then he calls for reinforcements. If it wasn't personal, he'd have done that as soon as he saw the girl," Chris added from the other chair.

"He wants a capture for himself. He's not letting anyone else in," Hernandez said. She still had on a space suit, but had taken the helmet off. Her spiky hair was plastered down with sweat. When Anna looked up briefly, she was surprised at how pretty she looked with her hair out of the way.

"That's right," the captain said. "He's not going to call anyone until it's obvious he can't recover Anna. And then he's only going to call to prevent trouble with his superiors."

"Will they dock? We can do the same thing," Hernandez said and Anna gagged.

"She means to get at their ship when it's undermanned and blow the docking clamp, Anna," the captain said, sounding very maternal. Anna nodded, still staring at her shoes.

"They will not dock," the computerized voice said, from a little speaker on the front of a tablet. Anna looked, just for a second. Mei Lin had changed into an old Fleet surplus uniform, by the looks, and her wet hair was freshly showered.

"Why?"

"They saw what happened to the other ship, drifting away dead in space. Apologies, Anna," the computer voice said. "A poor choice of words."

Anna looked up to see Mei Lin looking at her with a genuinely sad face. She had thought she was being teased at first, since it was so hard to tell what the monotone voice meant. "Thank you."

"He won't board and he can't risk shooting us. What does he do?" the captain asked.

Anna looked up. "He can't risk blowing us up, captain. He could shoot us all he wants."

"Good point, cadet. Then why hasn't he?"

"Fear," Chris answered. "He's more afraid of hurting the girl than of missing out on his prize."

"If that's true, then why?" the captain said, looking at the room but stopping her gaze on Anna. "What makes a pirate behave?"

"He's not a pirate," Anna answered. "Not to himself."

Mei Lin nodded, barely, but the rest of them just looked at her. The captain waited a moment and then nodded for her to continue. "You see them as petty thugs and criminals. They think they are the law and the strong methods they use are what is required against the lawless types outside the Fleet."

"Sounds like standard academy training," Chris sneered. Anna and the captain both nodded.

"So what scares him is someone up the chain of command leaning on him to make sure he recovers this fugitive in one piece," Anna concluded.

"That's about three dozen Fleet officers who might have said something to him."

"I think we need to contact Admiral Cosgrove," Anna said.

Iris Belmonte went pale. The rest of the crew looked surprised.

"How did you know?" the captain asked.

Anna looked at her in surprise. "Know what?"

"Everyone, get to battlestations and stay ready. Chris and Dan, please wait outside. Mei Lin, you stay with me."

They looked at the captain and grumbled a little, but everyone cleared out of the bridge. Iris waited until the door sealed and clicked into a locked position before looking back at Anna.

"Admiral Cosgrove. Spill."

"I don't know what you mean, captain. She's the one that would put that sort of fear into them."

"Why her, Cadet? Why did you go straight there? To the former supreme commander?"

Anna's brows closed together in surprise. "I sort of figured you knew already, Captain. She's my mother."

Iris laughed. Behind her, Mei Lin shook her head, a big smile on her face, but she didn't make any noise. "I wondered about all the Fleet chatter, but we hadn't heard that part of the missing girl story yet."

"I didn't want to say because I wanted to stay hidden until I could figure out what was safe."

"Mei Lin, please code the communications," Iris said. The smaller woman hopped over to that station and began punching buttons. The main screen dissolved into static, from where it had been watching the Dragoon ship float nearby.

The image resolved into the logo of Fleet Command. As soon as it did, Iris stood a little straighter and pulled at her civilian clothes, trying to straighten them some. She saluted when the image changed to a thin woman with precisely styled blonde hair.

"I don't have the time, Commander Belmonte," the Admiral said in the curt voice Anna knew well. Anna looked in surprise at Iris, who was still saluting. "I have about five major emergencies on my desk. Although I was about to call you on one of them."

"Thank you, Admiral. But I wanted you to know I have recovered Anna."

The admiral's eyes grew wide. Anna waved at the screen and at first didn't know if she was in range. Then her mother's eyes narrowed to dark little slits. That was also a look she knew. "There is going to be hell to pay when you get back to the academy, Cadet," she said in that neutral voice Anna feared most of all.

"Yes, ma'am. I can explain."

"I'm sure you can spin a wonderful tale, Anna. Hopefully one that explains four people wounded and huge damage to our landing pods."

"I...," she started.

"Not now. Commander Belmonte, I will recall the forces looking for Anna. But you need to get her to a safe place very fast."

"About that, Admiral. We engaged a force of Dragoons that boarded our ship. There were casualties."

"Your crew?"

"No, Admiral," Iris said, with a trace of pride. Anna could hear it in her voice.

"I'll deal with it, then. I trust Lieutenant Nakamura was involved?"

"Yes, admiral."

"Mei Lin," the admiral growled. "You're a half step away from life in prison, yet again."

The Asian woman nodded and gave a little bow to the screen, her face covered by a large frown.

"It'll take me longer to clean this up than I expected, then. Iris, you need to keep Anna safe."

"Will do, Admiral. We have a routine supply run for the rest of the week."

"Not anymore. Listen carefully. She stays aboard the ship and has no contact with anyone. You leave a pilot with her so that she can get back if you screw this up, understood?"

"What are we doing, Admiral?"

"Fugitive recovery, Commander. Is your team still battle ready after today?"

"More so than ever."

"I'm sending the files to your server through the usual anonymous channels. Review them and get in motion quickly."

"Will do. Understood, ma'am."

"A word of caution. There is another team in the field."

"Fugitive recovery from Fleet Security?"

"Covert operations from Fleet Command."

"A vast difference, Admiral."

"Not for a trained team, Commander," she said in that curt way. "And keep my daughter safe or you answer to me."

Then the screen went to the Command logo and back to the

Dragoon ship without any more ceremony. Iris looked at it for a moment, then turned to Anna. "You stay ten feet or less from me at all times, unless I tell you to stand by someone else."

"You're not a merchant ship, are you?"

"No bonus points for figuring that one out, after seeing the Admiral, kid."

"Who are you?"

"You heard her."

Anna shook her head. "I know your name. But what is this?"

"It is a covert operation," Mei Lin said through the tinny voice of the tablet speaker.

"Fleet Command?"

"Of course."

"Like the team that you're competing with?"

"Maybe. Maybe not. We never know who else is in the field. Or who they work for. There are as many factions in the Fleet as ships, they say," Iris added.

Iris hit the button on the side of her chair. "All crew to duty stations. Prepare to depart in two minutes." As soon as she said it, the door was open and the one-legged man and spiky-headed woman rushing to their stations.

Mei Lin moved closer. Anna shivered a little and the smaller woman stopped. She tapped her tablet a few times. The voice was much quieter when it spoke. "The captain and I are the only ones fully in the know. Everyone else is former service that hired on to work for us."

"And you work for my mother?"

"Since the day I was assigned to her flagship ten years ago," Mei Lin said.

Anna nodded. Then the silence stretched.

"I better strap in," Mei Lin said after a moment, her sad eyes watching Anna in a way that made her feel bad. Anna just nodded.

"Course is now going to the computer," Iris said from across the way, watching the pair of them as they parted. "Strap in, Anna. And don't unstrap or think about unstrapping until I tell you."

"Yes, captain," she saluted. Babysitter or not, she couldn't help but smile as she was going into space for the first time on a mission, even if it was just as a spectator.

Chapter 26

Gannar looked up as he heard the heavy doors sliding open. They only opened a hair, the old hydraulics grinding their dry parts together, before slamming closed again.

"That's not a very defensible position," Sergei said, his little feet carrying him without a noise across the room.

"Being far from here is the best defense I can think of," Gannar said. "What's that?"

The boy slung the pack off his back and pulled the woolen cover back. The woven basket was almost his size and Gannar had to sit up to look into it. He beamed, then scowled, his hand diving into the basket.

"Where did you get this?"

"Salvage," Sergei said. "Can you use it?"

"This isn't salvage, Serg. I've been on this planet six months and I've never seen anything this good."

"So it will work for your project?"

Gannar looked at the box he had torn open, with wires and green circuit boards cluttering the floor. He pulled a piece of wire out and compared it to the copper piece in his hand. "It's a perfect match."

"Great. What's our ETA?"

"It's a perfect match, Sergei. You disappear for an hour and show up with fiber optics and copper filament conductors that match a very distinctive type of wrecked ship. That's not coincidence. Or salvage," he finished, as he saw his little brother's mouth start to say those same words.

"You're doing a full dental exam on a gift horse, Gannar," Sergei said. He pulled off his little travel cloak and tossed it into the corner. That was as close to housekeeping as Gannar had been able to push him.

"Just because you're an amazing little genius, I'm not looking the other way. Spill."

"Salvage."

Gannar held up the cable, then fished another piece out of the basket. "This one is marked FF321. That's a code for the Fleet shipyard at Nova Halifax. This one is imprinted, right into the copper, with the call sign for a Fleet Attack and Reconnaissance ship. So…salvage?"

"Salvage doesn't just mean I pulled it from one of the wrecks at the dump. It means I salvaged it from another ship."

Gannar jumped to his feet. "Fleet Security? Here?"

"Relax," Serg said, walking to the little water fountain on the wall of the wreck and sipping, as his brother stood and stared. "It's not Fleet Security."

"A transport? A pirate?"

"Fleet Command Covert Ops, I think. The sort of special forces they deny they really have."

"Don't joke."

"I'm serious. A four man assault squad. Armed to the teeth. And a fifth that looked oddly familiar."

"No games."

"Your half-brother Sephalos is with them. Wearing a little tactical suit and everything. It's so cute," he mocked.

"He's taller than me, Serg. I doubt it's little. Or cute."

"It sort of is. The way the bumble around and miss the target by a mile."

"Where are they? How long do they have?"

Serg shook a hand in front of his face. "Don't worry. I put them in the landing tunnels under the city. We'll have a day before they get out."

"You put them? The generator?"

"Of course. You didn't expect hand to hand with all five of them, did you?"

Gannar took a deep breath. He put his hands to his head, pushing the thick hair back. It bounced back into place immediately. He scratched at the side of his face. "You just confirmed to them that we have the generator."

"They are pretty stupid if they didn't know it was gone," Sergei said with a giggle.

"The Fleet knows. Steve probably heard rumors. But the men with guns didn't know, until you used it and my brother filled in the pieces."

"Is he that smart?"

Gannar shook his head. "While no one has anything approaching your ego or intellect, little brother, yes. Even if he didn't know beforehand, traveling a mile in a heartbeat by teleportation would fill him in."

"Hmm," Serg said, rubbing his little chin. "I guess you better get that drive unit working again. Fast."

"You think?" Gannar said, grabbing a handful of wire and sliding back under the broken box of computer pieces.

"I'll get some supplies and be back in an hour."

"Try not to declare war on the Separatists and the Fleet while you're at it."

There wasn't an answer, just the grinding of the doors opening and clanging shut. Gannar exhaled, blowing all sorts of dust down into his eyes, as he patched the new cable into the places it had torn free years ago. Leaving wasn't a goal now. It was the only option and one that was on a fast approaching deadline.

Chapter 27

Steve waited as the rest of the team wandered the perimeter around the emergency shelters, noting landmarks and drawing the boundaries of camp. The four little tents didn't look like enough, but they were guaranteed by the less covert forces to be reliable. Steve drove the last of the stakes in, admiring his work, as the other men returned to the little circle of rocks and tents.

"The boulders will provide some natural cover. It's at least a mile to the next structure, as far as I could see," Sunderland said, pointing in the direction he'd seen something. "It'd be easier with binoculars, of course."

Mayberry just shook his head. He'd been quiet the last stretch, limping a little on the rough rocks. Steve had tried to talk to him, but he'd barely answered. "Let it go," Mayberry said after a moment.

"How does a team go into the field without basic equipment?"

"I fly the ship, Sunderland. I don't pack the bags."

"Don't go blaming me," Morris spoke up, from where he was leaning against a rock and rubbing his hands over the red rocks. "I packed everything on the manifest."

"So apparently Mr. Sunderland failed to list them as a necessary item?" Mayberry gloated.

"This isn't getting us anywhere," Lao said quietly. He'd built a little pile of rocks and sat in the middle of it, his rifle perched and ready.

"You're on watch, Airman. Let the big boys deal with this," Sunderland barked back.

"Don't go pulling rank," Morris replied quickly. "This is a non-hierarchical operation."

"It's the Fleet, Morris. What part of that means rank doesn't apply?" Sunderland snapped.

"The part where we signed the statement that rank didn't apply when we volunteered for this," Mayberry started in, before Sunderland had even finished. "Or else I'd be the senior officer and we'd already be back in space."

"So you know where to find him?"

"I know not to get taken by some tiny con artist."

"Be quiet," Steve yelled. They all looked at him, either in surprise or ready to keep arguing.

"Big mouth on a little boy," Sunderland laughed.

"I'm a team member, you said. So I'm telling you this isn't acting like a team. Or helping our goal."

"Cadet, don't get ahead of yourself," Sunderland said, turning to face Steve. But Mayberry put a hand on his chest.

"Point taken, Cadet. So what should we be doing?"

"We have a camp. We have about an hour of daylight, I estimate. We need to get some food and tuck in. Dawn will be here fast and we need to get back to the city."

"Which way would that be, fearless leader?" Sunderland said. "If you can tell through your innate intelligence without binoculars."

"I can't. Which is why we're waiting for morning instead of wandering the rocks like fools in the dark."

"Kid has a point," Morris said. "The team lost one today, not any one of us. We didn't know the enemy and we walked into a trap."

"We're lucky to be alive," Lao said. "Some people wouldn't have let us walk."

Mayberry and Sunderland glared at each other a moment. Steve watched them, anxious. Then they both sighed and nodded, almost like mirror images. "We are lucky," Sunderland said. "Apologies, gents. I don't like seeing the prey get the better of us."

"So what's our plan for tomorrow? Everyone?" Mayberry asked this as he sat in front of one of the tents, stretching out his long legs. Sunderland followed a moment later. Lao kept watching the perimeter, but the rest of them gathered around Mayberry's small wrist template.

"Can you get a signal yet?"

"Not enough to locate our ship. There's a ton of iron in these rocks and it's bouncing the signal back and forth like crazy."

"Will we know when we start walking?" Morris asked.

Steve nodded and Mayberry followed suit a moment later. "These tunnels are high in iron, but the rest of the plain looks pretty well covered in trees. There should be less interference out there where the soil hasn't been churned."

"And what do we do when we get back to the ship?" Sunderland asked.

"We see if we have any record of the kid in our files, which I doubt. A rugrat on a halfway independent world isn't going to be properly registered or identified."

"And when we don't see him? It's a city of at least 15,000 people," Morris asked.

"We had one chance at surprise and they saw us coming. So we make ourselves obvious." They laughed a little.

"I don't get it," Steve said.

"Recovery tactics 101. We'll show you," Morris said, patting him on the shoulder. Steve smiled along with them, still not sure why but it definitely was great to be one of the guys.

Chapter 28

Anna sipped from the bottle of water Mei Lin had handed her. She was glad she'd eaten, even with the constant dips and flares of the ship's gravity as they spun in orbit. She was also glad she hadn't been rude when the small woman brought a tray, although her first instinct was to flinch and her second to get sick again.

"Staring at the screen won't get us there faster," Chris said from the helm, turning back with a smile. Anna could tell the woman was checking on her, probably on the captain's orders, from the way she glanced at the center chair as she talked.

"If it did, our return trips home would take about fifteen minutes," Iris added, looking up from the papers she'd been signing and handing back to Hernandez. Hernandez had her hair molded back into numerous spikes. It had been flat and long after she'd taken off her helmet and space suit. She'd added bright purple eye shadow, too, which clashed with the blue of the uniform she was wearing. It wasn't any sort of uniform Anna knew. It certainly wasn't a regulation look. Anna couldn't figure out if it was a cool look or wrong that it was so different than what a crew should wear, according to the academy. This whole ship was confusing like that.

"We'll reach a stable orbit in about fifteen minutes," Chris said from the helm.

"How's the traffic, Carlos?"

The one-legged man clicked a few buttons, enhancing the image on the screen. The brown planet was striped with white clouds. A few silver sparks blinked across the screen. "Next to nothing. A navigation satellite is pinging."

"Where's the other ship?"

"Nothing is showing up."

"It may have been a lander that's on the surface," Chris suggested.

"I'd prefer I knew what I was looking at."

"We do too, Captain," Carlos said. "No one likes going in blind."

"Get scanning for something on the surface. If we can locate their ship, we know where we're putting down."

Carlos nodded and went back to staring at the monitors on his console. "There's only one spaceport capable of handling an interstellar ship. They are silent. And we're not picking up any ships."

"It's a breach of Fleet regulation 123.2 for a ship to deactivate the permanent beacon," Anna added, almost automatically.

"Do you think we're missing it, Cadet?" the captain asked. Carlos looked back at her for a second, then went back to tapping the screen.

Anna thought about it for a moment. "No, ma'am. I didn't mean you were missing it."

"Are you giving me that answer because you believe it or because you reconsidered?"

"I'm sure your people know what they are doing, captain. I was just surprised an official rule was disregarded. By a team on a mission."

"The rules get broken a lot, cadet. I wish they taught that at the academy."

"It's not as sheltered and theoretical as people think, captain. We do learn a lot."

"I'm sure. So did you learn what to do about a hidden ship we need to locate?"

Anna beamed. "Unless they've pulled it from the ship, yes."

Carlos spun around and this time he was looking interested. "What do you mean?."

Anna walked over, surprised by how her legs prickled and stung. She didn't realize she'd been sitting still so long, staring at the screen. "Do you have a dual transponder?"

"No, we're a hundred year old garbage scow," Chris grumbled from the next chair.

"So set it to single mode and broadcast code 3321, then flip it back to dual."

Carlos looked at the captain, who nodded. He snapped big fingers over the keypad, then waited. Everyone looked at Anna as silence hung over the bridge. "Nothing," he said.

"Are you sure you got the code right?" she asked.

"Reconsider that question, cadet," he growled, almost too quiet to hear. The look he gave her made it pretty clear he knew what he was doing.

"Let me check something." Anna walked to the far side of the console and pulled open a metal hatch. With a creak, the metal plate came off the front of the panel and she sat in front of it, studying the insides of the navigation station.

"Don't hit anything that keeps us from going home," the captain said, her voice light. When Anna looked up, the serious look in the eyes didn't match the tone. Anna pulled back, sure that she was going to be told to stop. The Iris nodded. Anna returned the look and reached back into the wires.

"Can I get a screwdriver?"

"How about a knife?" Carlos said, drawing a six inch blade from his belt. He handed it over, handle first. Anna felt her eyes got big when she saw it. The handle was soft leather. At the tail of it, set into the base of the handle, was a round little coin.

"That's the Silver Cross," Anna said.

"Check the blade," he smiled. She looked and then moved it further away, studying it. The image of a ship was laser engraved onto the metal. It was faint, probably to keep from weakening the blade.

"That's the <u>Kennedy</u>. My mom's ship."

"I think the Fleet would say it was theirs, but yes. She was the executive officer when I was there."

"You must have been young."

He smiled again. "Just a junior enlisted man when we went into battle. Then I became a former enlisted man with half a leg."

"How did you get the Cross, though?"

"Console first. Then talk," the captain said.

Anna looked down into the innards again. She traced one of the blue wires, to where it ran into a block of white wires. "Let's see," she said to herself, looking at it. Then she slid the knife into the white wires and pushed.

Anna held up a white plastic block, with wires trailing off it. "This belong to anyone?"

"What is it?" Carlos asked her. Chris leaned over his shoulder, looking. The captain's eyes narrowed from the command chair.

"That better not be a signal blocker," Iris said.

"It is, captain," Anna said. She didn't know whether to be happy she'd done something surprising or upset along with the crew, as their faces fell.

"Resend that code," Iris ordered. Carlos saluted and punched the numbers into the pad.

"Two signals, captain," Carlos said. He sounded confused.

"What?" Anna asked, leaning over his shoulder.

"We had pings from two Fleet ships on the surface. The computer doesn't recognize either, but they are Fleet ships."

"What did you do?" Chris asked, still leaning over Carlos to watch Anna.

"A beacon has a permanent link to the power source. It can be made to identify itself."

"Clever. Perhaps academy leaning is good for something," Iris added.

"Something practical?"

Iris smiled, just a tiny upturn of the corners of her mouth. "Not that I'm happy to know we're dealing with two Fleet ships."

Anna turned back to Carlos. "The Cross?"

"I was a member of a gunnery crew. Our ammunition was sabotaged and I helped clear it off the ship as it exploded."

"That sounds familiar."

"It's a shame more don't learn about it," he said with a little sigh.

"Later," Iris said, sounding more serious than before. "Two ships. Tell me something."

Chris looked down at her screen, then called Hernandez over. The two women with spiked hair consulted in low voices. After a moment, the helm operator turned back. "One of the signals is weak and old. I don't think it's a new arrival."

"I can't imagine an old ship would be here and not be picked clean."

"It may be. The mechanical pieces involved are tiny and built into the frame in some places," Anna chimed in, moving back to the chair on the side of the room.

"Smart, kid," the captain said, leaning forward in her chair to look at the screen. "Can we identify the types of ships at all?"

"The codes aren't anything our ship recognizes," Carlos said. "They may not be in the official registry."

"Can you do any more magic, kid?" the captain asked.

Anna smiled. "Sorry, captain. All I knew was how to make the transponder talk."

"It's good to know going in that there are two Fleet ships," Hernandez said. "She earned her keep this trip. We might want to keep her."

"Maybe if we ever have an opening," the captain said. She smiled when she said it, but it lasted just a second. "But all of you dress for business. I don't want any vacancies." Anna lost her own smile as she realized what a vacancy meant. Someone would be dead if there was a space to be filled.

Hernandez saluted. Next to her, Chris nodded. Carlos tapped a quick code on the keypad and the screen shifted to the locations that were broadcasting. "Less than a mile from each other. What's our insert?"

The captain studied the two little yellow lights blinking on the screen. She tapped the armrest, staring between the two. "Go for the new one."

"Are you sure, captain?" Anna asked.

"You have something, cadet?"

"Besides insubordination?" Chris added.

"I'm sorry. If that's what the other team used to reach the planet, it's probably guarded."

"And probably closer to their target?"

"I hadn't thought of that," Anna admitted after a long pause. "I'm sorry, captain."

"It's ok, kid. You're still in school. When you're commanding, you can go anywhere you want."

"I don't think this is something they teach."

"In some ways, they do. And the rest of it you'll pick up."

"Plus, the captain could be wrong and the other signal could be exactly what we want," Hernandez added.

"Very true," Iris laughed. "Suit up, people. Hernandez, you and Mei Lin are the advance team."

"Is that safe?" Hernandez asked.

"It's what I said."

"No offense, but the kid gets to question crazy orders. Do we want Mei Lin on the planet?"

"I want her armed and watching your back, Vida. She's combat trained and very angry. That's what we need if this is a fully armed combat team on the ground."

"And what do we do if it is?"

"That's why we're going hot," the captain said. She tilted her head just a bit toward Anna, but she saw.

"I understand what you're saying, captain. You don't need to be gentle."

"You're a kid, cadet. You might understand but that doesn't mean I'm going to say it in front of you."

"Understood, ma'am."

"Don't go all icy and cold on me. We still need your help."

"How? I'm confined to the ship."

"No question there. You're staying here and staying quiet. But this white thing you pulled out. Explain it while they are getting ready."

Anna looked at the little block of plastic in the captain's hand. "Well, I'm not the tech expert my brother Steve is. But it looks like a standard frequency modulator."

"What's that mean?" Iris pressed.

"Certain codes are getting scrambled when you try to send them. Like the code to make a Fleet ship respond."

"Why?"

"I don't know."

"Are there other codes?"

"I don't know," Anna admitted. "My dad taught us that one. I think he taught Steve some more. Making lights blink or something. It had to do with the Separation Wars and I never really got into that."

"Wish I could say the same," Carlos said from the front of the room. The captain gave him a very cold look. "Sorry, captain," he said after a moment.

"It's ok, cadet. That's a heck of a lot more than I ever knew," Iris said. Then she stared at the block for a few moments.

"Shannon," she said, turning to the communications station, "get Luis on the line."

Chapter 29

"Won't that give us away? Our position?" Anna asked. She sat fast, barely catching the edge of the chair. Her heart raced even faster at the thought of the just-missed fall and how embarrassing that would be. Like the memories of the Dragoons weren't bad enough.

"We're long outside their jurisdiction."

"But...the fight...," Anna said, trying to make a sentence out of all the thoughts in her head.

Iris Belmonte waved her to silence as the screen fuzzed with static and resolved to a Fleet logo. Anna was trying to figure out which division it was when that disappeared and the dark interior of the Dragoon ship was back on screen.

Luis stared at the camera a moment, his red eye glaring and reflecting on the lens and distorting everything. "My salvage crew just found a mess I'll have to explain to HQ. Care to fill me in?"

"I don't know what you mean."

"Major Andrews and team appear to have met with an accident. Their ship was forcibly depressurized and blew free from the docking clamps."

"Accidents do happen."

"And the part where a few violent men met violent ends, floating loose outside of the ship?"

"Maybe they were still in their ship. Expelled by the decompression, perhaps. I've seen it."

"Captain, you're one of the few people I'd believe when they say that. If you cross my jurisdiction again, though, you'll experience it."

"Idle threats, Benjamin."

He sighed. "What do you want, Belmonte?"

She held up the little white box. "You know what this is?"

His red eye moved. Anna felt her stomach twisting a little. It felt so wrong to see a human body butchered like that. And that thought brought other memories back and forced her to stare at the glowing red light and try to forget. "Your camera resolution isn't good enough for me to pick up a serial number, but it looks like a standard three resistor frequency modulator."

"More than I could tell you, Luis. Pop open your console by the transponder and see if you have one."

"We shouldn't," he said, pointing off screen. He was quiet a moment and Anna could hear the scraping of boots, and then metal, in the background. "We do."

"It's scrambling transponder codes."

"Why?"

"For one, as our little cadet tells us, code 3221 will make any other Fleet ship in the air ping."

He waved a hand again, then smiled when a quiet voice said something to him. "You just made my job a thousand times easier."

"That probably makes us even, then."

"For Andrews? Not at all. If I ever see you again, I'm shooting first." He said it with a smile that made Anna uncomfortable. It was just as friendly as the rest of the conversation, but she felt how serious he was. Then the screen went black.

"They cut communications," Shannon said.

"Why would you tell him, Captain? When he wouldn't agree to leave us alone?"

Iris gave a little tap to her head. "He may have a machine in there, but he doesn't think that far ahead. His bosses will catch on very fast and then we'll see what happens to him when a ship starts using that code all the time."

"So it was a trap for him?"

She sighed. "Sort of. It's complicated, kid. We were at the academy at about the same time. We know some of the same people, although we weren't friends. We're on opposite sides of the same side, I guess you could say."

"So you knew he wouldn't forgive...what happened?" Anna heard the catch in her voice and grabbed the edge of the chair. She willed herself not to remember the things she'd seen and fought to keep from crying again.

Iris sat down on the edge of the little bench. Her arm was heavy, but comfortably so, as she put it around Anna's shoulders. "Kid, don't think too hard about what you saw. It was bad. Real bad, for a kid. But there's a lot of bad stuff out there."

"Knowing there's more doesn't make it less bad."

"No. But you have to start putting that fear and memory in a special place. Come back to it later. Because either you obsess about it and burn out, or you learn to ignore it and you're less human than our metal-eyed friend. Never forget, but don't always remember."

"Thanks, captain."

Iris stood. She grimaced a little as she did, her knees cracking. "And never spend two years in zero G, because your body will never adapt back to gravity. That lesson is free," she smiled.

"Noted," Anna smiled back.

"Luis wouldn't let what happened go. Not because he really cares. Because we made him look bad."

"So why did we call him?

"Because he's probably the person least allied with us who would still take my call," Iris said. "If the same thing was on his ship, it wasn't his people that did it."

"Who are all of these people you talk about? The behind the scenes people?"

"Fleet Command, mostly. Just like there are separate covert ops teams. Some people have built their own private armies, basically. Preparing for another Separation War."

"But it's the Fleet. We're unified now..."

"We were then, too, kid."

Anna was quiet. She didn't have anything else to say, as the captain and the communications officer both gave her sad looks. She felt like a little baby in front of them, saying something stupid again and again.

"We're ready, captain," the call over the speaker crackled, breaking the little silence. Anna looked up, with a start at the sudden noise.

Iris stepped back, closer to the command chair, and hit the big white button again. "Ok, Hernandez. We'll come down at a barely legal speed. You folks be ready to spill."

"Locked and loaded, captain," the tinny voice called back. Then the static stopped as red lights flashed around the bridge.

"Automated warning," Carlos said, looking over his shoulder at Anna. She'd tensed and just about jumped out of her seat.

"We're exceeding suggested entry rate," Chris said. "We'll be on the ground in about five...four," she counted. Anna watched the view change as they moved. The arc of the planet disappeared into a brown blur, striped with white clouds. The clouds were suddenly all around them and there was a grey stripe on the ground.

"Two," Chris said. The stripe was now taking shape as a stretch of buildings, of all difference sizes, growing up around a long landing strip.

"One," Chris said, slowly, hitting switches. The ship rocked in the atmosphere. "Down!" She yelled this last one, hitting the hatch release keys. The buildings now towered above them, or at least were at their level. A bunch of human shapes were in the distance, behind a blast shield, waiting for the ship to dock.

Anna watched the two figures sprint out of the lock. Both were wearing black suits she recognized as tactical gear. With the suits, they'd have resistance to a lot of weapons and computer ties to the ship's systems. They ran, making the surprised dock workers jump back behind their shield. Anna almost laughed, from the surprised expressions she could just make out on the men's faces as the ship's cameras zoomed.

Mei Lin reached the ship first, which surprised Anna. She'd lagged behind the whole run, then sprinted with churning little legs at the last few yards. The small woman slapped something silver onto the bay door and kept moving. She'd barely stopped to slap the thing into place. Hernandez hit a second later, throwing another item, this one dark grey, as she spun off to the side. Both took cover behind a stack of crates.

"Echo active," Shannon said. "No noises."

"Give it a couple," the captain said.

The silence on the bridge felt heavy. "Still nothing," Shannon said, pressing the earphones tight to her ears.

"Appears empty," Chris spoke into the microphone she'd just pulled out of the central console.

"Triggering," Hernandez called back. One of the things stuck to the door smoked. The darker one, that she'd put in place. Mei Lin had placed the listening device and Hernandez the dangerous one. Anna was somehow happier to see that. The two metal squares smoked and fell to the ground and door fell outward. The two women moved toward the ship, slowly this time. Mei Lin stuck the silver piece back into her belt pouch. Both had pistols out now. Not stunners, because there wasn't hull pressure to worry about. Heavy metal weapons that just looked dangerous, even through the screen.

"Careful," Iris cautioned, talking to the screen. The two women reached the door and slid in carefully. "Helmet cams," she ordered.

"On," Hernandez said. The screen switched from the outer view of the ship to a head-height image of a dark corridor.

"Carlos, make sure you keep eyes on the outside of that bird. I want to know if anyone even looks at it," Iris said. The man nodded, looking at a smaller screen built into the console. "Vida, commentary, please."

"It's some type of attack ship I haven't seen before. One bunk room with a head and shower, then a bigger room with eight flight chairs and storage."

"What are we looking at now?"

"Bunk room. Let me get lights," she said, and the room lit. "Helmet cam isn't so good in low light."

"Looks like packs for five guys," Hernandez said. "Uniforms on the ground, so they are probably wearing tacticals."

"Any sign of weapons?"

"Mei is pointing toward the main cabin. Hold on," Hernandez said, as the camera moved from the duffel bags to the smaller woman. Hernandez moved back out into the bright cabin, with the comfortable looking chairs and the walls full of doors. Mei Lin went straight to a big square panel on the wall and pulled the handle, opening out a long door. It hung from the wall on chains, so it stopped at 90 degrees, like a little desk. Except the wall behind and the little flat surface were lined with felt-looking material and the shape of various weapons.

"Four Armin auto pistols. Two Gerzek machine pistols. Possibly three to five explosive charges."

Mei Lin had moved on, opening up another cabinet. This one was even longer, but had the same felt when Hernandez turned her head. "Space for two rifles, but there isn't any identifier. May be Fleet MX-184 rifles, at a guess."

"So we are looking at a heavily armed assault team."

"No question, Captain."

"Movement," Carlos yelled. Everyone tensed. The camera even jumped as Hernandez pulled back. She and Mei Lin slammed the cabinets shut and drew their weapons. Watching through the helmet cameras, Anna felt like she was right with them. There was tightness in her chest. She tried to fight it, but there were tears on the edges of her eyes. She could feel them hanging there, just waiting to start the flood. It wasn't just the unknown. It was knowing what Mei Lin had done and knowing she might see it happen again.

"Hold on, just a kid."

Everyone exhaled all at once. "Don't do that to me, Carlos," Hernandez said over the microphone.

"He is heading right for you, though."

Anna felt another tightness. "Let me see," she said, rushing up to the main console. Carlos tipped the screen so she could have a better view.

She knew the kid. Tiny, with a mop of blond hair. It was weird, but it relaxed her somehow to see that face. "I talked to him before. He hacked my tablet, at school."

"He did? He looks about six," the captain said, leaning over her shoulder. "He's smarter than you Cosgrove kids, if that's the case."

"That hurts," Anna said, with a pretend sniff. Everyone relaxed a little with her joke. "What's he doing?"

"I don't know," Carlos said. "He's walking in like he owns the place, though."

"What do we do?" Hernandez had moved closer to the door. Mei Lin was on the other side of it. They were trying to stay back and out of sight, but from the edge of their view Anna could see the shadow approaching.

"Hold steady. It may be a false alarm," the captain said. Anna looked at her in surprise and Iris shrugged.

"He's heading for the cooling rig," Carlos said. "Yep, he's pulling the coolant loops." On screen, everyone watched the little kid use very quick hands to unhook the cover and start pulling out the lengths of metal pipe. Each rod was almost as tall as he was, but he quickly assembled a stack of them on the ground. "Huge resale value in those, since coolant can't be sold legally anywhere outside Fleet stations." The kid pulled out some elastic wraps and started bundling the rods together.

"So we have a six year old hacker slash thief looting a Fleet ship? I want in on this," Iris said. "Hernandez, change in plans. We're going to want to talk to this kid."

"Understood," she said. The helmet cam moved as she walked down the narrow hall and stepped out the broken door. There was a flash to her side as Mei Lin moved, staying in the shadow and hugging the side of the ship.

"Freeze. Fleet Security!" Hernandez said, rounding the corner.

The kid stopped, his eyes big. Anna felt the face looked very familiar, and more than from just seeing him once before. The hair and eyes reminded her of someone. He had a backpack on, with eight of the rods crammed in, and another two in his hands.

"You're not Security," he said after a moment. His demeanor changed, too. His shoulders slouched back and his eyes went back to the same slight squint.

"You're stealing from the Fleet."

"Of course I am. It is how we get by here."

"We're taking you in."

His eyes flittered around. Then he smiled. "How lazy of me. I didn't see the door before. You're not exactly invited guests, are you? Despite your fancy suits."

"Put the rods down and come with us," Hernandez ordered. Mei Lin took a step forward and he skittered back.

"What happened to you?" he asked, staring at the face with the scars. Anna saw Mei Lin's face out of the corner of the helmet cam and felt her tears welling up again. The look on Mei Lin's face was absolute grief. "Sorry, I have places to be."

"Grab him," the captain barked. Mei Lin darted forward, but he was already moving.

The red lights flashed on the bridge again. "Captain! We're picking up something weird."

"Mei Lin, Hernandez, do not pursue. Something," the captain started to say, then the lights stopped and it was regular yellow-white light.

"It was an energy signal that triggered the system," Carlos said. "It tripped every alert code we had, including some I've never seen. It was sort of like the transponder trick the cadet taught us."

"Anna, do you have any idea what that was?"

"No," Anna lied, shaking her head. She felt the tears building up even deeper now, circling her whole eye. So it was true that Jeecey had been a thief and a traitor when he ran away.

Chapter 30

"We should be on the move."

"It will be dark in a few minutes."

"You've been saying that for half an hour."

"It's at least an hour back to the ship."

"So we walk a bit in the dark."

"Open to hostile threats?"

"What threats are there? One man who sees in the dark just as bad as us."

Mayberry rolled his eyes and shrugged. Sunderland and Morris were on the edge of the camp, attempting to argue in low tones. It wasn't working, in part because the rest of the area was so quiet.

"They know we can hear them?" Steve asked, much more quietly.

"Probably. Heat of the moment, though."

"If the Fleet has the planet on lockdown, he's not going to be able to go anywhere. Off planet, I mean," Steve said.

"Sure, but there's a lot of empty space outside of this city. A smart man could live off the land for years," Mayberry replied. "If he leaves the city, we've lost him."

"Now that we know he has the generator, though, he won't have years. There will be four battalions on the ground as soon as we radio in," Steve said. Mayberry looked up then and Steve fixed him with his most earnest glare.

"You're wondering why we haven't called this in?"

"Yeah. This is huge."

Mayberry nodded. He looked at where Lao was scanning the space around camp, then at where Sunderland and Morris were talking. They were quieter now, closer together but their hands were moving fast. The discussion was still happening. "We were told something big might be involved. Orders were to ignore it and continue with mission objectives."

"I think this is bigger than that."

"If it were up to me, I'd agree, Cadet. Explicit words from Major Morris were that no matter how big we think something is, it's not big enough."

"So we're supposed to gather him up and haul him back, regardless of whether or not we recover one of the most dangerous tools ever invented? That's...," Steve started, and Mayberry raised a hand as his voice started to climb.

"That's an order, cadet. You know what I learned over a year as an officer? It's better to follow the order you're given than to do the right thing."

"That's ridiculous."

"Can't argue with that," he said, standing up as Sunderland approached.

"Mayberry, Morris is ready to storm off and travel through the night."

"Morris," Mayberry called out. The man stopped, where he was jamming things into his pack, and looked up. "You can't go on your own. You'll blow what's left of our advantages."

"What advantages, Lieutenant? Sorry, it's Ensign now, right? The advantage of giving him time and daylight to head into the bush? We need this over, fast."

"We go in at daylight. We get civil authorities to help and we use standard police procedures. We'll have him in hours."

"He won't be there in hours, Mayberry," Morris yelled back. "He knows we're here. He knows why we are here."

"What can he do about it, Morris? Run? We have infinite manpower."

"Back home, sure. We need to complete our mission, Ensign. You have as much riding on this as I do."

The sky flickered. Steve hopped to his feet, watching the stars slowly shimmer and wiggle. "Wait," Steve started.

"Kid, stay here," Morris said. He threw his pack over his shoulder and picked up the long rifle.

"No, I'm not coming. It's the sky. The generator is firing up again."

Everyone looked. "I don't see anything," Sunderland said.

It flickered again. Steve turned to see their faces, hoping they'd see it. Open jaws and scared eyes told him they had.

"Everyone, grab the emergency gear. Get in close together!" Mayberry yelled as he dove toward the tent, throwing provisions and water tanks into the open door. Lao was a step behind him, ripping down another tent, then a second. He balled them up and threw them to Mayberry, who jammed them into the standing tent. "Stay close and hang onto your gear. Everyone you're holding will come with you!"

"He's not running. He's making us run!" Morris yelled. He turned and started running. "I'll meet you at the city!"

"Morris, wait!" Sunderland, Mayberry and Steve all yelled. Then the sky went black again and an awful silence overtook everything. Then Morris screamed. Just for a moment, just the start of a horrible yell.

"Morris!" Mayberry yelled and started to move, but Sunderland grabbed him. Mayberry pushed back and Sunderland's grab turned into a bear hug. Steve grabbed, holding Mayberry by the waist.

Then the world flickered back to reality. This time it was a city street. Little adobe buildings and huts of scrap metal ran on both sides of a dirt road. Sunderland let go and Mayberry took off.

He didn't have to go far. Steve could already see Morris. Or what was left. "The generator bubble caught him," he said, because he had to say something. Someone had to fill the silence.

"Cost us one of our good rifles, too," Sunderland said a moment later. It was true. Most of Mayberry's left side was completely gone, from the waist up. The rifle was also cut in half, laying next to him. Steve turned to look at Sunderland, not believing, but then he saw the shocked look. Sunderland was just filling silence too. For the first time, Steve noted that the man he thought of as a commanding officer wasn't more than five years older than he was. The day's growth of beard on his face was two little blonde patches, far less than Steve's own.

"Regroup," Mayberry said, storming back over. "We're down one. Our most experienced soldier. We get back on plan. Get back to the ship," he said, pointing to the silver towers not far in the distance, "and get the civil authorities."

"What do we do with Morris?" Steve asked. He didn't want to look when he asked, but had to. He was surprised to see Mayberry had thrown a blanket over the pair of legs and foot of torso that had come through with them.

"Remember him for being a good soldier. For now, we keep moving. It's only a mile or so to those towers and we have time to get there now. So throw everything into a pack and get ready."

"We stay close," Sunderland added. "Cadet, you keep an eye out for signs of that weapon. Yell if you see anything. Lao, you have point."

The airman nodded, moving back to the lead point. Steve fell in beside him, grabbing a collapsed tent as soon as Mayberry jammed it into a pack and handed it over. Five minutes later, they were moving slowly down an empty dirt road, leaving one of their own behind.

Chapter 31

It was dark when they reached the edge of the landing field. The silver towers of the few modern buildings were still far in the distance. It had only taken a half hour, but Steve felt like it had been hours.

"Urban travel is terrible," Mayberry acknowledged as they paused in the shadow of a hut for a quickly passed canteen. "So many places for threats that we move at a crawl."

Lao had crawled out of the shadow, moving on his belly. Steve watched him stand, matching the shadow being thrown by a directional beacon on the edge of the runway, then he was gone. "He's good," Steve whispered after a moment.

"Exceptional skills in some areas. Sadly lacking in others," Sunderland answered, from where he was watching their backs. "That's how we all got picked for this team."

"Including the skill of getting in the way," Mayberry joked, giving Steve a little tap on the shoulder. They both laughed, just a little chuckle, very quiet. Steve felt sad to laugh, with Morris on the ground not too far away, as soon as the sound left his mouth.

Lao crawled back a moment later. His black suit was very good camouflage in the shadows around the paved landing strip. "There's another ship in our landing berth. Looks like a commercial freighter."

"Double docking is illegal, but common," Sunderland said. "The port can't refuse landing fees."

"More than that," Lao said. "The door has been cut off our ship. It looks like it's been looted."

"That's insane!" Mayberry said, and everyone shushed him. "Sorry. Who would interfere with a Fleet ship? That's treason."

"Sounds like a good opening line to me," a woman's voice said from the dark. Sunderland jumped, grabbing for the rifle he'd leaned against the wall. It was gone. Mayberry and Steve both jumped up, going for their holsters. The two weapons that pointed back at them made Steve forget about the stunner instantly.

The two women facing them wore tactical suits, although they looked worn and a little out of date. The pistols they carried were top of the line automatic projectile weapons.

"Those are our weapons," Mayberry pointed out.

"Not anymore, Ensign," one of the women answered. Steve was a little startled, and it took him a moment to see why. He'd seen civilians all his life, but he'd never seen them in uniforms carrying weapons. Both women had fairly short hair, but twisted into braided spikes that stood up in all directions.

"Rights of salvage," the other said, in a softer voice.

"That's piracy."

"No, someone else blew the doors open and carried most of the engine off. We just came across a disabled ship and exercised our rights."

"You can't mean," he started. Then the third one came out. She was small. Her eyes were Asian, as was the skin tone over most of her exposed face and hands. The red welt that ran from the collar of her tactical shirt, across the throat and then up past her ear, was a stark contrast to her smooth skin. She was carrying Sunderland's rifle. Her eyes were dark and angry.

"The Peace Accords of Camp David," Steve said. He was babbling. He was filling space because the little woman scared him so much. He didn't know why. Something about the look in her eyes made him sure she would kill him without hesitation. "Any disabled ship abandoned for more than a day without a notification beacon is classed as salvage."

"You're a lawyer now, too?" Mayberry sighed. Steve turned on him, a little hurt at the tone. Mayberry just raised a hand in surrender. The Asian woman raised her rifle, too.

"Where's the gunman?"

"Who?" Mayberry asked, before he saw the woman was looking at him, but not talking to him. Her eyes flickered briefly over to the Asian woman. She ran a finger across her throat.

"Lin!"

She shook her head. Fast, and repeated.

"They mean Morris," Steve said, filling the space again. "She didn't do it. He was caught in the bubble of the..." He stopped, feeling Mayberry's grip on his shoulder tighten to painful.

"The what?"

"Doesn't matter. He's dead," Steve said, looking down.

"Bad planning to send a kid that soft on a removal mission," the gruffer woman said.

"Wasn't our original plan," Sunderland replied.

The shorter of the spiky woman kicked a little metal box forward. It grated on the asphalt as it tumbled the few feet to Mayberry. "New plan. All of you put your weapons and communication devices in the box."

"Fleet ID too," the taller one said. "It will all be returned once we're ready to leave."

"We're against a deadline here," Mayberry added, although he was unstrapping the wrist tablet as he said it. "This is a very dangerous man we're after."

"No question, Ensign. Too dangerous to let you get him when there are things the Fleet needs to know."

"You're Fleet?" Steve asked, in surprise. The little Asian woman almost smiled at that.

"Used to be. Private contractor now," the shorter one said. The other two didn't say anything, but motioned them into action with their weapons. Steve felt oddly undressed as the stunner fell into the metal crate. He felt absolutely naked as he pulled the academy ID chips from around his neck and dropped them in.

"Kick it back," the shorter woman said, as Sunderland dropped his pistol and a knife into the box. He gave it a little shove and it traveled about half the distance. "More," she said.

Sunderland sighed in frustration and took a step forward, aiming his back foot for a big kick. Except when he went to plant, he just kept going and dove at the woman.

There was an electric crackle in the air. Sunderland shook on the ground, his whole body shaking with spasms. It took about ten seconds before he stopped moving and another ten for his eyes to open.

The little Asian woman still held the rifle, one handed, and had a bright yellow military stunner in her other hand. She covered Sunderland with it, preparing for a second shot.

"Santos, lock that box," the taller woman said. The shorter spiky haired woman stepped closer, keeping an eye on Sunderland. He watched her, but his arms and legs kept moving on their own. He wasn't getting up after that shot. She closed the lid on the box and tapped it with the wrist tablet she was wearing.

"You two will have to carry Mr. Hero here," the woman said after a moment. "You're carrying this box. And don't get any ideas," she said to Steve. He nodded. "It's code locked and you'd need a full AI system to break it. Just cooperate and you'll spend a few hours in a brig before we never see each other again."

"I'm ok with that," Steve answered, as Lao and Mayberry lifted Sunderland. He was taller than both of them and his feet sort of dragged even though he was trying to walk.

"Guess you're the one of them that hasn't been there before, then," the shorter one laughed. Steve turned to see what she meant, but she motioned with her pistol. He started walking, following the limping threesome, with the armed women at the rear of the little convoy.

Chapter 32

"Why does a merchant ship have a brig like this, anyway?" Steve asked.

They'd been in the room about ten minutes. Darkness had set in on the walk back, short as it had been, making the place even darker to navigate. It had been hard for them to help Sunderland, although he was mostly recovered as he lay on the room's lone bunk.

"Easy guess would be they aren't merchants, kid," Mayberry answered. He was using the room's toilet as a chair, leaning back against the wall.

"I'd guessed that part. I was trying to figure out who they were."

"Meaning?" Sunderland said. He rolled over, grunting with some pain, to look at where Steve had balled up a blanket on the floor.

"Former Fleet. I'd say that they are well-trained, to surprise a covert operations team in the field. And then they have a top-of-the-line brig on a fairly old freighter."

"Fugitive recovery," Lao suggested. "Going where the Fleet can't, to recover deserters."

"That's what I thought," Steve said. "But I can't figure out why they'd send two of the same team."

"Well, that depends on your definitions," Sunderland said.

"Enough, Ensign," Mayberry said.

"He's a part of the team. You said so yourself, Mayberry."

"What's going on?" Steve was confused by the sudden tension between the two senior officers.

"They may be fugitive recovery, but we're not a typical team, Steve," Mayberry said. "We've been pulled from different teams working near your family."

"Cosgrove specialists?"

"Yes."

"No," Lao said. "Trilouis specialists."

"I'm not sure what there is to learn that isn't in the files. He had no real family and no friends, as far as I know." Steve paused as he talked, trying to remember anything about his half-brother that would be useful.

"As far as we know, too," Mayberry said. "But we worked hard to know that. I was reassigned to the academy, to watch you and your sister. You're both good kids."

"I'm from Fleet Command Auxiliary Services," Sunderland said. "I was busted down after a blowup with another officer and I've been working as an assistant in your father's offices."

"Sharing stories?" Lao said, leaning back on his own next of cushions. "I've been doing a ten year sentence at Penal 4 on the Moon.

My roommates were several of his co-conspirators from the <u>Eagle</u> job. Before that I was with special forces."

"I didn't think there were survivors," Steve said. Then he nodded. "I know. That's what we were supposed to think."

"Right in one, kid," Sunderland said.

"And Morris was from Fleet Marines. He'd been in action a dozen times and lost his commission over some of them. He served with Admiral Cosgrove's ground forces for a time, but that wasn't why he was brought in."

"The gunman, she called him. He was to kill Gannar."

"No," Sunderland said. "He was the point man on a mission this team was assigned. Any of us were to follow through on that objective."

"Why? It's a stupid plan."

"Like you've had brilliant moves so far kid? I don't know why. I follow orders. Maybe you can ask Morris."

"If he hadn't been..." Steve started. Sunderland sat up, ready to fire back, but Mayberry waved them both down.

"Shut up, both of you. Don't take this out on each other because we're in a bad place. Morris was killed by a combination of his own stupidity and because an enemy used a powerful weapon against us. Both are to blame, and I don't care to hear any more."

"Yes, sir," Sunderland muttered, sarcasm hanging. Steve just nodded, staring at his shoes.

"Relax, kid," Mayberry said. "It's not going on your permanent record."

"Yeah," Sunderland said. "Sorry, guys. This thing is getting to me. I'm not being professional."

"Isn't that cute," a voice laughed from outside the brig. They all turned, quickly, to where the little blond boy was watching them.

"You!" Sunderland steamed, but he didn't get up. Mayberry was on his feet, but no one else had moved.

"Yes, me. I'm guessing you big bad guys want out of this jail?"

"Don't joke around."

"Would I have crawled through fifty meters of air duct to get in here if I was kidding? They haven't changed those filters in a year. Good thing I have had my allergy shots."

"What do you want?"

The kid pulled a bag forward, from where it had been on the ground behind him. It made a heavy metal sound. "I want to create discord and mayhem."

"Meaning?" Sunderland glared.

The little boy sighed. "Do I need to download a dictionary for you?"

"Don't be smart. You're aiding a criminal and could be in big trouble."

The kid had a high short laugh. "At this juncture, our normally opposed worldviews have aligned. I need you out of this cell."

"I think that's a reason to sit tight."

"All well and good, then," the boy said. He reached out and set his hand on the keypad next to the door. There was a brief hum and the brig lights flickered, then the door locks clicked open with a big metallic noise. "Of course, now that the door has been opened, there's about a thirty second window before they rush down here."

"They'll find us waiting patiently."

"Suit yourself." The little blond boy shrugged and walked away, turning the corner and disappearing from view on silent feet.

"Waiting patiently? With a story about a little kid that opens doors with his mind?" Sunderland said. "They'll think they caught us at something."

Lao moved first. He was on his feet and out the door, grabbing the brown bag. He looked inside and pulled out two projectile pistols. "If I complete this mission, I don't go back to Penal 4. I don't know what they told you guys, but it's worth it to me."

"Lao, don't...," Mayberry started. The hiss of air from the elevator opening filled the air.

Lao turned and fired. The gun roared in the little hallway. Steve blinked out of pure instinct and ducked from reflex as the huge noise and bright light filled the hallway.

"Move, move," Sunderland yelled, pushing from behind. Steve started to resist, then Mayberry grabbed him and yanked as he ran past. Lao blocked one side of the hall, holding a heavy pistol in two hands, so they ran the other way. Mayberry kicked open a hatch and slid down the ladder. Steve followed, feeling the skin on his hands burn as he tried to slow the skid down the rungs. Sunderland came fast after him, one of his boots catching Steve on the side of the head as he jumped off.

"Sorry kid," he barked. "Keep moving!"

Mayberry was already moving, down another hallway, with Sunderland close behind him. Steve took off after them. The whole ship was filled with the echo of running feet, as boots smashed metal decking.

"There's the kid!" Sunderland yelled, his boots squeaking as he tried to change course. Mayberry turned to motion and then the hallway filled with another blast of light and sound. Steve fell, trying to remember the training. He kept rolling, trying to get to the side of the hall.

Lao dropped from the ladder, jumping the last half. He landed with a cry and raised his pistol immediately, firing two shots back into the floor above. Then he was up and running. Steve saw the blood flowing from wounds to his arm, but couldn't see what it was. Steve started to get back up but new boots were coming down the ladder. He looked down the hall, but it was too far to run. He ducked lower, behind some unmarked shipping crates. The space was small and he felt greasy dust, meaning it hadn't been cleaned in a very long time. His neck hurt from trying to bend so low, behind the box, but he heard footsteps racing by and that was enough to make it not as bad. He stood, after letting the silence sit for a minute. The hall looked desolate and empty after all the action.

"You're not really a part of this, are you?" a woman asked.

Steve spun, raising his hands. It was one of the spiky-haired women. Without the other one there to compare, it took him a moment to recognize the softer-voiced shorter one. "Not really."

"Why don't you go back upstairs and I'll lock you in. You stay there and cooperate."

Steve looked down the hallway, where his team had run. There was blood staining the metal tiles, where Lao was dripping as he ran. In the distance, he heard the electric crackle of stunners. "Yes, ma'am."

"You go slowly, and I'll be behind you. Up the ladder."

Steve nodded. The metal rungs burned his sore palms as he tried to climb. It took a moment, his arms and legs shaking, before he was able to get the strength to move.

"Not that slow," the woman said.

"Sorry. This is...scary."

"Not the adventure you imagined the Fleet would be?"

Steve looked over his shoulder as he climbed. She was on the ground, a stunner pointed up at him. "Nothing like it at all."

"Me either, kid. That's why I was out after five years."

Steve reached the top of the ladder and climbed back out. Another woman with a rifle moved to cover him, so he raised his hands as soon as he could.

"What did you do in the Fleet?"

"Not chat time, Chris," the second spiky-haired woman said, her rifle locked on Steve.

"Chatting prisoners are rarely shooting prisoners, Vida," she answered as she reached the top of the ladder, drawing the stunner from her holster again, although Steve had already walked back into the cell.

"We didn't escape," Steve said. "I mean, someone let us out. A little blond kid."

"That's a new one on me," the one named Vida said.

Chris pushed the door shut and punched in a long string of codes. "Now it's going to take either my hand or a major unlikely event for this thing to open before we reach port."

"I'm ok with that," Steve said. "I think my dad had the right idea in working at the spacedock."

"And miss all this?" his original captor said, with a smile. She'd reholstered her stunner.

"What are you going to do with my team? When you catch them?"

The two women looked at each other. Steve felt his heart race as he waited for an answer. "Separate cells at the civilian jail until the Fleet comes to get them," Chris said after a moment.

Steve didn't believe them. He saw they looked at each other, probably thinking that the look on his face was pretty clear. Then Vida disappeared through a hatch, away from the brig.

"You stay here and you'll be okay. That's the thing you need to remember."

"Will do," he said, sinking onto the bed. It had been Sunderland's personal territory not ten minutes ago.

The spiky-haired woman took a step toward the hatch, then paused. "I was a Marine Nav tech," Chris said after a moment.

"Excuse me?"

"I joined the Fleet to do all those things the recruiting posters promised. Get an education, see the world, grow up."

"Did you?"

"Yeah. I just didn't like who I was growing up to be. So I finished my contract and went to work for a private firm that pays me well for navigation skills."

"Sounds like the Fleet trained you well."

"Sure. I've navigated routes that the top pilots in the Fleet still copy. Except I was always be in a support role since I didn't have an Academy degree. There are a lot of good officers out there, but they don't see the pyramid holding them up."

"It's too bad they missed your talent. Exceptional...," he started.

She laughed. Her smile fell when she saw his face. "Sorry, kid. I didn't mean to be rude. I'm better than average, but not exceptional. I'm just another cog in the system. That's what I didn't care for. "

"I don't get it. You signed up for the tour."

"That I did. That's what my dad said when I said I wasn't reenlisting. Out here, I work hard enough I'll own a ship, or be a partner in a ship. Back home, the most I had to look forward to was retiring at 40 with a Sergeant's rank and retirement fund."

"A lot of people would like that. It's service to all our people."

She shook her head. "I'm not badmouthing it, kid. It just wasn't for me. But you asked what I did, so I wanted you to know."

"Because chatty prisoners don't shoot?"

"Something like that," she said, with a genuine smile that lit her face. Despite the crazy hair, it sort of reminded Steve of Josette. He felt a flutter in his chest when he thought of her and the life he'd left back at school. "Sit tight and don't breathe too hard. We'll have someone watching the cell now."

"Yes, ma'am," Steve saluted, as she closed up the ladder hatch and locked it, then disappeared into the hallway where the other woman had gone.

Chapter 33

Iris took a key from around her neck and handed it to Carlos. He raised an eyebrow, but didn't say whatever he was thinking after she gave him a glare that stopped him before his mouth opened.

"What is going on?" Anna asked. She'd fallen asleep for a few minutes, sitting in the long bench on the back of the bridge. She yawned and stretched, feeling the cooler air of the night as the borrowed shirt rode up a little.

"We picked up some of that covert ops team, but now they are loose in the ship."

"That's not good," Anna said.

"Thanks, cadet. I hadn't figured that out," Iris said.

Carlos limped forward, using his crutch, and put the key he'd been given into a slot beside the main screen. He turned it and the bridge door hissed with added pressurization. "Locked, captain."

"I just sealed the bridge. You don't have anything to worry about," the captain said to Anna.

"I wasn't really worried. I figured you had it under control."

Iris smiled. "Thank you, Anna. Unfortunately, this is a bit worrisome. We captured the covert operations team, but somehow they got free. Our sensors went dead and they overrode the lock."

"Is everyone ok?"

"So far," Iris said. "The escapees are armed, however, and there have been shots fired."

Anna felt the tightness in her stomach and rocked forward. She hadn't expected it to be like that. These were Fleet officers, after all. "What do we do?"

"The rest of the crew is combing through the ship. Carlos and I are going to sit tight and try to track everyone's movements with the internal cameras. We'd like your help."

"Yes, ma'am," Anna said, getting to her feet. It helped the pain in her stomach to be moving. It kept the memories of carnage at bay, too.

Iris tapped a few keys at Chris's station and adjusted the monitor as it came to life. "This is the brig. One of the team surrendered. Keep an eye on him and alert me of anything."

"Like what?"

"If he does anything other than sit there on that bed, you let me know," Iris said.

Anna saluted, which earned a smile from the captain, and took a seat. The image was fairly grainy, of a man sitting on the bed, not looking near the camera.

"They aren't the best cameras," Carlos said, sounding like he was offering an apology. "We didn't think we'd be paying this much attention to the inside on a seven man ship."

"Seven? I thought there were only six."

"Right now. Hopefully we don't lose anyone before we get back to pick him up," Carlos said.

"Screen, Anna," the captain reminded. She was at Shannon's station watching a different monitor. "Hernandez, we have two men approaching your position."

Anna turned back to the monitor. The man had moved. She'd thought he looked oddly familiar when she was just seeing the back of his head and the flat black of a tactical suit. "Steve?"

"You know him?"

"That's my brother."

"What?" the captain called out. "Not you, Vida. Stay ready. About fifteen yards."

"Mei Lin, lock those doors behind you and keep heading this way," Carlos said. "Shannon, Mei Lin is coming up behind you in about ten seconds. She's the only one in your area, so be calm."

"Roger," the communications officer said in her sultry voice. "Then what?"

"Wait," the captain broke onto the channel. "Carlos, we've locked down two thirds of the ship. Where are they?"

"Right outside our door," he said, furiously pounding switches. A moment later, the room filled with echoes of blasts against the door. "It'll hold for a century, but we might get a little hungry."

"Can we depressurize like we did before?"

"We're not in space, kid," the captain said. "That trick only works if there isn't a vacuum outside."

"Sorry. You're right. Do you have sleeping gas or something?"

"Carlos, any ideas?"

He was quiet a moment, looking at the screen's grainy images. It went fuzzy with a big crackling noise. "They just caught our camera and took it out." More booms echoed as the door came under another volley. "We don't have anything like that can take someone out like that."

"Especially with a friendly aboard," the captain said. "He is friendly, Anna, right?"

"Of course. I don't know what he's doing with them."

"Being an officer in training. What cadet wouldn't want to be on a mission with some up and coming young officers?" Carlos sounded wistful as he said it, like he was remembering being young.

The captain nodded as Carlos talked. "I can see that." Her own voice reflected some of what Anna was sure she heard from the pilot. Iris looked over the communications board, then flipped a couple of red

228

switches. "You. In the brig."

Anna watched Steve look up. He looked a little confused, but she was glad to see he wasn't hurt. She'd feared bruises and broken bones. She saw his mouth move, but there wasn't any sound on her monitor. She could hear the crackle of a voice from the captain's spot, but it wasn't as loud as the other channels. She wished she could hear his voice.

The room shook again as something new hammered against the door. Anna spun, covering her ears, expecting it to be hanging off the hinges.

Carlos turned in his chair, using his cane to push off the console. "They are bursting oxygen cartridges. Not enough blast to do anything, but the echoes are going to be annoying. Probably what they are aiming for."

"Ok," the captain said, drawing Anna's attention back in. "Here's what happens, kid. I pop the brig door, you run. Straight to the spaceport cops. Get someone back here fast. Understood?"

Anna saw him nod. Iris punched a series of keys and waited. Nothing happened. "Hang on, kid," she said, shutting down the microphone. "The security locks are in place. I can't trigger it from here."

"Don't look at me. I'm not running down there," Carlos said, waving his crutch. Then he laughed as Anna stared at him in horror. "Relax kid. The legless guy jokes are funny when I make them."

"No one is running down there. We've sealed or trapped all the halls. The ventilation shaft isn't big enough for anything bigger than a child."

"So how do we get him out?" Anna asked, over the latest round of pounding on the door.

"Someone needs to work the door manually. He's going to have to sit tight."

"Captain," Carlos said, his voice rising. "Get down!"

Iris obeyed instantly. Anna took a moment longer, trying to see the monitor. To see what Carlos had seen.

The explosion rocked the ship. Anna felt a hot breeze, then it was hotter than she'd ever been. She saw the floor moving away, but the heat was so much she couldn't figure it out. Then the viewscreen was right next to her. She reached out with her right arm, only to watch the arm bend badly.

"Anna!" the captain yelled, jumping across the bridge in a quick leap.

"My arm!" she yelped as the captain started moving her. Carlos was right there a moment later, a medical kit in one hand. He grabbed the arm and yanked. Anna felt her throat go raw, but she couldn't really hear the scream she knew she was making. Her ears rang from whatever had just happened. He wrapped something around her arm and she felt sudden pressure, which took away some of the pain.

"It's busted. The emergency splint will hold it and numb it, but you're going to the doctor as fast as possible."

"What happened?" she said. Carlos dabbed at a spot of blood on her head, then helped her into a chair.

"They gave up on trying to blow the door and punched a hole through the hull. A big hole."

"So you can't lift?"

"The ship is almost falling apart. The hole is that big."

"Won't someone notice?"

"No one is going to come near two Fleet ships unless we go out there and tell them to," the captain said.

"We still can't see them, but the hallway cameras behind them show some more motion. Like they are doing a second charge."

"What for?"

Carlos looked at the captain, then back to Anna. "To speculate? They are going to blow the bridge off the ship. Without the power holding the door shut, then it's just a question of prying it open."

"That's pretty poor design," Anna said.

"Tell your father. This is a reconditioned Fleet freighter."

Anna smiled, just for a second until she remembered the men outside the door. Then her arm throbbed again and her face fell further.

"If I get home."

She noticed no one chided her or made sympathetic noises. Both just nodded as they studied the monitors and cycled between views. "Hernandez, Mei Lin. You're closest to the bridge. Get up here and chase them away before they blow us all up," the captain said. Her voice stayed level, but her manner was a lot more rushed than Anna had seen.

"Shannon, Chris, we need you to get that kid from the brig and get off the ship. Forget chasing the escapees," Carlos said at the same time.

"We have one cornered near engineering, Carlos. We can get him."

"We don't have time for prisoners right now. Get the kid and get off. Captain's orders," he said, and Iris nodded as he said it.

"We're moving," Chris responded. The start of whatever she said to her partner started to come through the speaker, then it returned to the softer crackle of dead air.

"So what do we do now?" Carlos asked. "I'm not aware of any super escape hatches in the bridges of these old ships."

"If I were a better pirate, I've had made one, I guess," Iris said back to him, with a little smile. "You have any ideas, genius?"

Anna shook her head. The whole bridge was creaking as the metal around them twisted under the strain of the explosion. "I never studied this sort of thing."

"That's the problem with the academy, kid. They'll teach you everything from the best books, but never the real life application," Iris said. "Not that most people would ever anticipate this, I guess." She got up and wandered the front of the bridge, looking at the viewscreen and the storage compartments along the wall. "What's behind the screen, Carlos?"

"Electronics, I'd guess."

"Standard hull plating beyond that, though?"

"Must be. Otherwise we'd have asteroids cracking into our heads twice an hour."

The bridge moved, shaking more than before. Everything tilted to the left from where Anna was sitting. She reached out with an arm, only to remember the break, and pitched sideways until she caught herself awkwardly with the left arm.

"We don't have much longer. Our team won't be up here for another few minutes," Carlos said. "Longer if they are taking fire."

Iris stared at the image on the screen, of the narrow space outside the door they could see with all the broken cameras. "So the hull plating is seamless. High tensile ceramic stuff. Keeps stuff out, but keeps us in right now."

"Air," Carlos said with a yell. "There's a vent underneath the bridge."

"Look! Find it!" Iris called, as she dropped to the floor. Anna followed, unsteady, as Carlos lowered himself on his crutch. They all crawled around, in silence other than the shuffling of hands and knees.

"Got something," Carlos said after a moment. He drew out the big knife and was levering the panel open when the other two reached him, still crawling. Underneath the panel was a thick metal grate.

"So close," Iris sighed.

"We're not done yet," Carlos said, poking at the edges of the grate with his knife. The first couple of times, there was a screeching metal-on-metal noise that made Anna feel like someone was poking her in the brain. Her hearing was still muffled but the sound went right through her. On the third one, the metal wobbled a little.

"Get your little hands under there," Carlos ordered, as he drove the knife in again. Anna reached in and tried to hook her fingers into the metal. It slipped away the first time.

"It's cold. And wet," she said, in surprise.

"Condensation from our landing and then sitting here," Carlos explained. "Again."

Anna reached in and got her fingers into the metal as Carlos pushed. "Good!" he called, "now pull." As she pulled, he wedged the knife back into the panel and pushed.

"The blade!" Anna said, watching it bend.

"Pull!" Carlos said, just as the blade snapped. The handle went flying out of his hand as the blade fell down into the shaft. Quicker than she could follow, he jammed his fingers in and started working the grate loose.

"Got it," he said after a moment. It didn't come all the way out, but he could pull enough of it to the side. "Anna, Iris, go," he barked. Outside the door, there was the sound of gunfire.

"Can we...?" the captain started, but he shook his head. Anna knew what she was asking, but her officer was right. There was no way to know who'd win in the hallway. This was their chance. They couldn't wait longer and hope their people resolved things and let them out.

Iris dropped first, jumping down so only the top of her head was visible. "It's tight, but it's a clear shot to the hull."

"Anna," Carlos said. She looked over at him and he nodded, so she jumped in.

The tunnel was tiny, barely big enough for Iris, right ahead of her, to crawl. Anna slid on the metal tube as she knelt and started into the duct. Up above, there was the sound of crashing metal. Anna looked up, half sure she was going to see rifles pointed down at her. Instead, there was Carlos. He had the handle of his knife jammed into his belt and was using his crutch to hold the grate. He skipped down, landing on his one foot, and yanked the crutch as he landed. The grate not only fell back into place, but the panel above it clanked down.

"Wow," Anna breathed.

"It's all leverage and levers. Basic physics. You academy kids aren't the only ones that learn this stuff," he said, but he was smiling. He leaned his crutch forward and levered himself down, then started sliding behind her on the slippery metal.

"I'm at the exit," Iris whispered back at them a moment later. It was a far shorter trip than Anna had expected, only a matter of yards, lengthened by corners and turns.

"There should be handles around the top and bottom edge," Carlos whispered from behind.

There was a loud clank. They all stopped, waiting to hear something follow it, but there was just the echo of whatever was going on above. With all the metal around, Anna couldn't hear anything except thumps and booms. "It's off. That was easy," Iris said.

"Exterior hatches are always simple. Cuts down on ground crew time cleaning and prepping for flight," Carlos said, giving Anna a push. She nodded, which made her feel silly since he couldn't see her head. Then more thumps and booms happened above and she increased her speed.

Iris was on the ground outside, reaching up. Anna grabbed her and fell face first through the hole. The captain grabbed her in strong arms, lowering her the few feet to the hot black asphalt. "You did landing field work?" Iris asked.

"Of course," Carlos said, hauling himself out of the tube. Anna was surprised to see the thick ropes of muscle in his arms as he caught himself coming out and flipped around to land on his foot. A moment later he pulled out his crutch, then pointed away from the ship. "Those cargo containers will be a good place to regroup." He took a step, and then the fireball filled the sky.

Anna saw red, then white. Black stars swirled in front of her face, then black pavement as she skidded to a stop. She could feel the blood on her face and her hands. She sat up, looking around, unsure of what was happening. Her broken arm filled her whole brain for a moment, then the scraped hands from where she landed. The pain faded as she stared at where the ship had been.

The bridge was on the ground. In the hole behind, two men with weapons were pointing. At her. They leaned out from behind cargo boxes, aiming at the ground. The shipping container jumped and shook, pieces of it being chewed away by gunfire.

Anna tried to get to her feet. With one arm already broken, it took a couple of tries. She looked around. She saw Carlos a few yards off to her right, beside the ship. "Captain!" he called. Then Anna saw the feet. Long, thin feet, in combat boots, sticking out from under the metal. "Anna, go!" he barked as she started toward him. Anna paused, just about falling in indecision.

She saw one of the men turn and get ready to jump, only to have his chest explode. She wanted to scream as his body fell. He still tried to grab his gun as he landed on his back, but Mei Lin leaned out of the hole and fired two shots. She saw more gore explode into the air.

Anna fell. It was all she had the energy to do. She fell so she was sitting, the shock running up her body. She started as she saw the other man by the crate look out at her. Ensign Mayberry. She knew him. She wondered what he was doing here, and then she saw Hernandez drive a shoulder into the box he was hiding behind from the other side. He scrambled, but man and box fell out of the hole that had been the ship's hallway. He landed awkwardly, his gun falling a few feet away, and before he could do more Chris and Shannon were next to him, weapons ready.

"Look out!" Anna heard Carlos yell. Another soldier leaned out of the hole in the side of the ship. Chris fell, blood spurting from her shoulder. She and Hernandez both returned fire, diving for cover, but the man had disappeared back into the ship.

"Anna, go!" she heard Carlos yell again. Somehow it reached the reflex centers of her brain, the ones she knew the academy was teaching to obey orders. She felt woozy as she started to move, but she got to her feet and ran for the distant shipping crates that offered safety.

Chapter 34

Steve held his breath, trying to cut down every noise he could control. He was sure he'd heard more gunfire, getting closer. Then the whole ship rocked and he gulped air, grabbing the side of the bunk to steady himself.

"Bad time to be resting, kid," a younger woman said as she appeared around the corner. She was heavier than most people he saw on Fleet ships, with a short dark haircut not out of place in places he'd usually be seen. The scattergun she was carrying was definitely not regulation, though.

"Captain's orders," he responded.

"Which captain are you listening to now?" she asked, keying in a long series of numbers on the keypad. The door beeped when she finished the first set, so she started punching in another long string of keystrokes.

"Whichever one gets me off here without getting shot," he said.

"Is that an honest answer?"

"Yes, ma'am."

"Smartest thing an academy kid ever said," she smiled, as the door chimed and Steve heard the metal bars slide open. A moment later the security lights went off and the door swung open on its own.

"What are we doing?" he asked.

"You're walking. I'm keeping anyone from shooting you in the interim."

"No one," he started, when gunfire exploded across the hallway. "No one is trying to shoot me."

"Accidents happen when fire is live, kid."

"Understood," Steve said. Morris hadn't been shot, but it felt the same.

"Stay down," she said, pushing him forward. He crawled and she followed behind, staying low and keeping the gun aimed at the narrow doorway. It was only a few feet and then Steve felt her hand pushing him through, into the bigger room beyond.

Steve stood as the woman pushed the metal door shut and used the manual locks to seal it up. "That won't hold for long, but it's something," she said. "You ok, kid?"

"I'm fine. What are you doing?"

"Getting you off the ship."

"I can talk to those other soldiers. I can get them to stop."

"I doubt that."

"They aren't here for you. I can get them and get on with our mission."

"Try not to use the 'our' when those guys are shooting up my home, ok, kid?"

"I have a name, you know."

"I assume you do, but I don't really care," she said, pushing him forward.

Steve grabbed at the gun as she pushed, turning away with a pivot. Then the butt of the gun caught him upside the head. He stumbled back, holding his aching eye.

"Dumb, kid."

"I'm a Fleet cadet. You can't hold me prisoner."

"You're a kid who's using Tactics 101 against a ten year veteran. Try again when you shave," she said.

Steve nodded and walked where she pointed. He slowed once, in the long silver hallway, and heard the sound of the weapon cocking behind him. "Don't get smart, kid. I'm supposed to get you off the ship for your safety. If you don't want to be safe, I have a crew I can be helping."

"Helping fight against Fleet officers?"

"Walk," she sighed.

Steve turned a corner and was surprised to see the hallway end. The hall was cracked and torn, blackened by fire. "What...," he started.

"Your friends," she said, pushing him toward the hole.

Steve stepped closer, looking out. Then the sound of gunfire echoed around him and he dove low.

The woman was crouched, angling the gun up and swiveling around. "Hop down," she said, not looking toward him.

"They are shooting."

"Better get away then," she said, and the gun swiveled toward him. Steve nodded and hopped the few feet out of the hole. The asphalt was hot as he hit, crouching to absorb the impact.

"Steve, move!" he heard someone yell. He looked over. Mayberry was on his back, his legs bent at an odd angle. He was waving a pistol up at the other side of the hole, divided by a wall, where a woman was leaning out with a rifle.

He looked for a moment and ran to Mayberry. He heard a gun fire somewhere and waited for pain, or nothing at all, but the only thing was the pounding of his feet on the asphalt.

Steve grabbed Mayberry's arm and yanked, trying to keep moving. His shoulders burned as he pulled, but then Mayberry got his feet underneath and pushed off. Steve dragged and Mayberry shuffled, keeping his weapon aimed back at the ship. The pair of them crossed the black paving, diving behind one of the long yellow cargo containers.

"You okay?" Steve asked.

Mayberry fell back against the container, breathing hard. "Not at all. I shouldn't have moved," he said, squeezing his legs and trying to straighten them out. He grimaced with each movement, punching the container and grimacing more. "But now I'm alive to worry about it. Thanks, kid."

"We'll get you to the medic," Steve said, looking around the corner of the container. "No one is coming after us."

"Someone's coming that way," Mayberry said, "or else I'm hallucinating."

Steve turned and looked. There was a silver vehicle moving toward them at a slow pace. "That's going to take a long time," he noted.

"Civilian cops aren't going to rush into a firefight."

"There are injured here," Steve said.

"Really?" Mayberry laughed. Then he grimaced again and sucked air in. "Maybe you should wave them down."

Steve edged forward, keeping an eye on the wreckage of the freighter, then stood long enough to wave. He dove back fast and the thump from hitting the container echoed. "Did they see me?"

"They changed direction. And picked up speed. Good job," Mayberry said. Then his eyes rolled back and he started to drool, his white eyes staring out.

"Mayberry? Ensign?" Steve asked. He shook the man, gently, until

Mayberry gulped in a big breath of air. His eyes didn't move, though, even when Steve shook him again.

Steve kept his hands on the man's shoulders. He didn't realize he was doing it at first, and felt embarrassed when he noticed. The feel of someone, not shooting at him or locking him up, was great. "I wonder what Josette is doing now," Steve said to himself, watching the big silver brick of a vehicle roll closer. He thought about his classes, with all the work he'd be required to make up and the potential for all the trouble he'd be in from classmates and professors for missing required work.

"Raise your hands," the mechanical voice issued from the speaker on the side of the silver vehicle. A small slot on the side of the moved, and a rifle barrel poked out.

Steve did as he was told, standing, with a little crouch to stay below the top of the container. It was still a couple inches taller than him, but the noises from the wreck behind him were still going on and he didn't want to stand out.

"Identify yourself," the tinny voice said.

"I am Sephalos Wroclaw Cosgrove. I'm a cadet at Fleet Academy Alpha."

"You are a long way from home," the machine voice said. "Identify yourself."

"Him?"

"Not you again."

"He's...Mayberry. I don't know more. He's a Fleet officer."

"Ensign David Mayberry. One year veteran. Survived armed conflict on Somali Resettlement Colony 2 due to suspected cowardice. Reassigned to academy when he refused to testify. Assigned to monitor Cosgrove twins on behalf of Fleet Command."

"How do you know all of that?"

The windshield tint disappeared instantly. The little blond boy at the controls gave a little smile and a wave. "You!" Steve called, dropping his arms.

"Yes, me. It is good to see you again. Or so I suppose I'm supposed to say. I'll open the hatch. You get in and be quiet."

"Why should I?"

The kid punched a button and the rifle barrel swiveled to aim right at Steve.

"That's the main reason. The other one is that your only way off this planet is through me."

Steve was quiet for a moment, looking at the smiling face in the driver's seat. "I need to get him aboard. He's hurt."

"Of course. Get the door first," the little voice said, through the machine.

Steve hustled to the back of the van and pulled open the security door. It moved on its own after a moment, gliding on smooth tracks.

Steve moved back around, watching the gun barrel track him as he moved.

"Wait," the voice said, just as Steve rounded the front of the van. He turned, to look up at the boy, just as the gun barrel moved again.

"No!" Steve yelled, lunging forward, but it was too late. The powerful gun fired. Mayberry's body jumped, but he didn't wake up at all in his last instant. Steve fell to his knees, next to the man, holding him tight to his chest.

"Get up," the boy said. Steve looked back. The kid looked bored, if anything.

"You killed him!"

"The shock was already killing him. He broke both legs and then tried to run on them."

"He was alive until you shot him!"

"Ironic how that works out. Now get in."

"I'm not going with you!"

The gun swiveled a few inches to the side. "You get in or you die here."

"You wouldn't shoot me."

"I would like nothing better, Sephalos. But I need you alive. So get in."

"I refuse," Steve said, taking a step back. Then he saw the other little slot on the side of the silver van. He turned, getting his feet under him, when he heard the whine of the stunner powering up. "You can't carry me yourself."

"You'd be surprised, Sephalos. Now get in the back."

"Stun me," he shouted, as he braced his feet and leapt into action. He heard the crackle and smiled at the idle threat, and then yelled as the blast of electricity hit him in the back. Steve fought to make his arms and legs work together, but it didn't do anything. The yellow striped blacktop was suddenly right in front of his face before everything went completely black.

Chapter 35

Anna knelt behind the heavy crates, watching the action going on in the distance. The wreck of the freighter looked large, next to the attack ship. She saw Carlos for a moment, before he ducked somewhere inside the broken bridge, and she saw other people pointing and running around.

She waited only long enough to catch her breath, just a few puffs, glad for all the time she'd spent on the track. Then she was moving again, toward the small security huts and control rooms on the edge of the field.

No one yelled at her and none of the shots she still heard came closer. She looked back, briefly, to see people shapes moving around in the open spaces that had been hallways, with more people on the ground. A silver security vehicle was closer to the scene now. She hoped it was over for them and the people left standing could get help.

"Help me," Anna said when she reached the first little prefab building. It was a guard shack, or something like it, just big enough for a man and a chair. Except the chair was empty of everything except cobwebs.

She turned and ran to the next one. This was a bigger building, the door already ajar. And just as empty. She stopped and looked. There was motion where the two ships sat, and where the silver van rolled closer, but the rest of the field was silent.

"Is this place even a real spaceport?" she asked herself, watching the birds spiral overhead and listening to the shots echoing.

"It used to be. It's been empty for a year or two," a quiet voice answered.

Anna spun, dropping into the self-defense stance. The man who was watching her smiled, showing lots of white teeth, and moved into the same stance. "Been a few years. Want to spar?"

"Jeecey!" she cried, jumping into his arms. "It was terrible! Steve's back there. We have to help him!"

"I already sent someone to get him. It's ok. We need to get you out of sight before someone else starts trying to find you." He led her into the little building and pushed open one of the storage closet doors. Except inside wasn't a closet. A couple worn jackets hung from hooks, filling up space. The stairway that ran out the back of the closet was metallic and looked very familiar.

"Is that from a Fleet ship?"

"You're always curious."

"Jeecey, I know about the generator. You really did take it. I never believed, but..."

"Shh. First we get out of the way before any Fleet cowboys shoot us up. Then we deal with what's going on here."

"You can't do that, Gannar. I'm not a little kid."

Her older brother turned, giving her a look that reminded her a lot of their mother. It was weird to see such a serious look on Gannar's face. "When have I ever treated you like a little kid, Anna Elizabeth Wroclaw Cosgrove?"

"Never," she admitted, feeling like a baby. "But we can't just run away. There are people out there who are hurt."

"The local cops are already on their way. They have good medics."

"Not like Fleet doctors. We need to call for help."

"Even if there wasn't something to your generator fears, Anna, I'm not calling the Fleet down on my head."

She started to say something, but he turned and started down the stairs, stopping to look back at her after a few steps. "Get the door behind you," he said, then disappeared down out of sight.

Anna chased after him, pulling the old metal door closed. "We have to get Steve. I won't follow just because you say so. You can't order me."

"No, but I can remind you. You're too curious not to come after me."

They took about ten steps in silence. Along the wall, the panel lights barely lit the grooved metal steps. "I was right. These are Fleet steps. From an older cruiser."

"Why do you say that?"

"The design is something Dad worked on. My dad, I mean," she said.

"Yeah, I got that. Old Rene wasn't really a design sort of guy."

"You never said much about your dad when we were growing up," Anna said. "That might be the first time I've heard you say his name."

He nodded and covered about five more steps. Anna trailed behind him. "So you know the steps," Gannar prompted.

"One of his earlier jobs was accessory work on the Valiant class. Making the little touches and designs that would make it homier. The curled bars on the step edges are something he was proud of."

"Good memory for details," Gannar said. "You're right. There was a Valiant-class ship among the wrecks abandoned here. A lot of the parts were useful."

"Parts for what?" she asked, but he just smiled back at her and jumped down the last three steps in a big bounce.

"You were faster with that question than I'd thought," he said, reaching the grey door at the bottom. "I'd hoped to show you this right as you asked." He lifted up a metal cover, revealing an old fashioned keypad, and punched in a series of numbers. There was a distant hum and the door creaked open, letting out a stale, hot smell.

"It's a bit boyish in here," he grinned. "Bachelor digs and all."

Anna followed him in. It looked like he'd salvaged an entire ancient warship for this shelter. "This thing is gorgeous," she said.

"It is, isn't it? A product of another era. They put a lot of time and money into all of this wood and leather."

"Is this real wood?" Anna ran her hands along the railing at the back of the bridge. Near one end, it was heavily scored and broken. Under the dark finish was pale yellow wood. "It is wood!"

"Heavy as heck, too. These sorts of ships weren't ever meant to be in gravity. Well, they were meant to land once if needed, but there's nothing that will lift it off again."

Anna thought of the freighter that wouldn't lift again, but seeing Jeecey overwhelmed her. "So you made it your home?"

"One of many, Anna. What about you? You look so grown up in that uniform."

She looked down at the salvaged pieces she was still wearing. There were new tears in the knees of her pants and the moisture from crawling out the air vent had matted the jacket into a wrinkled mess. "Not the uniform I thought I'd see you in, though," he added.

"What did you expect? An admiral at 18?"

"Fleet Security," another voice answered. The little blond boy walked out from the bridge. A step behind him, looking a little green, Sephalos trailed. He stumbled a little when he walked and his eyes were glassy.

"Steve!" Anna yelled, rushing to him. She expected his usual strength but she bowled him over with her leap. The two crashed to the ground. Anna grimaced as the shock ran through her broken arm. Steve whimpered a bit.

"Careful!" he snapped a second later.

"What's wrong? Are you hurt?" she cried, grabbing his arms and then running her hands over his head, then shoulders, looking for injury.

"Stunner hangover," the little boy said.

"Sergei, I told you to bring him quietly!"

"He didn't want to come," the boy said, with a shrug.

"He shot Mayberry," Steve said, his voice sounding stronger.

"Dave Mayberry? He was here?" Gannar asked, as Anna covered her mouth in surprise.

"He had to be put down. Merciful, you know," Sergei said, with a frown.

"That's not," Steve started, but Gannar waved a hand.

"It's ok, Steve. I'll deal with this. You need to get some fluids and rest up."

"He shot an officer. On a mission. On duty," Steve said. Gannar nodded, but he didn't take his eyes from the little blond boy.

"Rest, Steve. We can deal with this when your head isn't splitting open," Gannar said, and Steve went even more green.

"Serg, go get a bunk cleaned up for him."

"Gannar," Serg whined, but Gannar shook his head. The boy stomped off, shooting daggers at Steve as he walked.

"Are you hurt, Sephalos?" Gannar asked.

"Woozy. Otherwise unharmed. Unlike the man your little psycho killed."

"You let me deal with Sergei. He's my responsibility. I will get you to safety first."

"There are injured people up there," Anna said. She stood, staring him down.

Gannar's eyes were colder than she remembered. A lot more sad, too, as he shook his head. "Anna, I already said. Local medical will get them. They have a good training program here."

"Gannar, they are friends. I can't leave them."

He sighed and closed his eyes. Anna was surprised by the lines around his eyes. She hadn't seen those the last time they'd talked. "I left a lot of friends over the years, Anna. It sucks, but sometimes there's no choice."

"You had a choice. You had everything. And you took a telephase generator with you," Steve said quietly from the floor. "You stole it."

"You don't know what happened back then, Sephalos. Let it go."

"We can't," Anna said, before her twin could speak. "We're Fleet cadets and we know you stole the most valuable piece of equipment in the Fleet. We have a duty."

"So you'd arrest your brother and drag me back to a military tribunal where I'd never see the light of day again?"

"Maybe not if there's more to the story," Steve said.

Anna looked at him in surprise. "He's right, Jeecey," she said. "Thank you, Steve."

"You know that there was an assassination team sent after him and you still think he's getting a fair trial?" Serg called from the other side of the room, leaning on the barely opened door.

"It wasn't an assassination team," Steve said. "It was a recovery team."

"Yes, it was, Steve," Anna said. "They were sent to kill Jeecey."

"Who told you that? Those rejects on the freighter?"

Anna felt her face go red and she clenched her fists. The pain from the broken bone interrupted her rage almost as soon as it started. Anna looked up at Gannar. It was like the old fights, she realized. She'd always turn to him when Steve didn't listen. "I'm not going to fight with you about this, because it doesn't matter," Anna said.

"You have intel you're not sharing?" Gannar asked the boy.

"Four man team, plus this one as a straggler. All of them brought in and offered good perks to make sure you didn't survive," Serg said.

"What sort of perks am I worth these days?" he smiled.

"Nothing new. Just the usual 'get out of jail free' or 'get your spectacularly ruined career' straightened out."

"How ruined?"

"You'd be a candidate," Sergei said. He gave a little smile that reminded Anna of her brother.

"That's spectacular, all right. See, that's an improvement. It used to be just the ones that got drunk at a party or something. They must be digging out losers with true potential."

Anna frowned. "It's not a joke, Jeecey. They are here to kill you!"

"Were here, girl," Sergei said, walking into the room and boosting himself up into one of the officer's chairs at the edge of the room. "They are all dead now."

Anna felt her stomach twist into knots. "And the people on the ship I came on?"

"One dead. Most wounded. They fought very well," Serg nodded.

"You are a very weird kid," Steve said, from his spot on the ground. He'd pulled himself to sitting, but still looked pale and weak.

"You don't know the half of it," Gannar answered. "I need to get

you two out of here and someplace where you can be picked up by the Fleet. They'll take care of you."

"You're coming with us," Steve said quickly.

"You can't even stand up, Sephalos. You're not threatening me."

"Good men are dead!"

Gannar held a hand over his eyes. His lips moved a few times, before he lowered his hand. There were wet streaks on the corners of his eyes. "You have no idea, kid. No idea."

"Is this about your Sarah? One woman dies and you throw away everything? Including our family?" Steve yelled. He tried to get up, but couldn't get a grip on anything with his shaky hands.

"Shut up!" Gannar yelled back. "No, it isn't about her. Or about those poor fools up above and the stupid chess games they play at Fleet Command with our lives. It's about making sure you don't die senseless deaths!"

Steve looked surprised. Anna felt she probably looked the same way. She's never heard him raise his voice. "You can't run forever," Anna added as the silence stretched. Gannar had his head in his hands. Steve still stared, his eyes angry. Sergei leaned back in the navigator's chair, his little boots dangling, a smile on his face.

"I'm not running, Anna. I'm getting ready to get out of this game."

"There is no game, Gannar," Steve said. "There are countless dead people who'd have lived with that generator aboard a ship."

Chapter 36

"So the Fleet picks a fight and loses, but it's his fault they lost? What about the person that picked the fight?" Sergei asked, crossing his legs and putting his hands behind his head. Anna almost laughed at the serious way he talked as he posed.

"The Fleet protects us all."

"The Fleet is a lie, moron," Serg yelled back.

"Enough!" Gannar said. He didn't raise his voice very much. It was more like Anna remembered. The strong and in control brother she always wanted to emulate. "Sergei, give us a minute."

"Why?"

"Because I need to talk to them."

"Do it with me here," he pouted. He crossed his arms on his little chest and thrust out his lip. Anna couldn't help but laugh.

"Protect me," Gannar sighed. Anna recognized the end of the old prayer mother had taught them. "Whatever, Sergei. Anna, Steve, listen to me. You're going home now. You're going to be good students and better people and work hard. Just like you always did. You're going to make your mother and father proud, or at least your father. I doubt you can work enough miracles to please her."

"What's this about?" Steve asked.

"Two things. I'm not going with you. I have things I need to do. And even if I didn't, firing squad isn't really on my agenda at any time soon."

"There's no guarantee," Anna started again, but she knew it wasn't true. Someone was sending teams to make sure he never reached a trial he could never win.

He just waved her off. "Second, the Fleet needs you. It needs good people who are smart enough to make decisions and think."

"The most brilliant minds," Steve started, but he stopped when Gannar raised a finger.

"Don't quote the recruiting fluff back at me. There are a lot of smart people in this galaxy outside your fleet. You can think whatever you want. About me, about what I did, about what the Fleet does. Just think. Okay?"

Anna nodded. She felt a tear rolling down her face and Gannar gave her a sad look.

"What's wrong, Annie?" he asked.

"This is the last time we're going to see you, isn't it? And we wouldn't even have this except for stupid things happening back at the academy."

"Serg?" Gannar asked.

"You said to get them here."

"So what did you do?"

"Soldier boy met up with some young guns who were his ideal of what officers would be. Rebel girl met some civilians who ended up bringing her on a covert ops mission."

Anna stared. "You couldn't have engineered this!"

Sergei smiled at her. It was a condescending look that made her want to punch him. And then she felt terrible, even though his little face was so smug. "The academy is a sealed system. Introducing the right variables was simple."

"You are an evil genius," she said. "You'd have to be."

He smiled and looked to Gannar, like it was a point for him in an ongoing game. A battle to see who was the best evil genius, she imagined. Except she couldn't think of Gannar as evil, despite everything that was going on.

"How are we getting home?" Steve asked. He was looking around the cabin and seemed bored already. He didn't want to be around Gannar, Anna knew.

"How close are we, Serg?" Jeecey asked. The little boy spun around and started hitting buttons on the console. Anna almost laughed at first, because the machinery was practically antique. She'd seen newer things in museums. Then the panel lights grew brighter and the lights flashed to full power on boards around the cabin.

"99.95%. Maybe point nine six."

"Can we give them a ride?"

"What are you talking about?" Steve asked. He'd pulled himself to his feet and was leaning heavily on the back of a chair. Anna felt the rush of bile in her throat when she saw the blood smeared across the tactical suit. Not his, but some soldier who'd died doing a job.

"You'd have to be an idiot to take them all the way home," Sergei said.

"How'd you know what I was thinking?"

"Genes," Sergei snorted. "You are an idiot."

"How old are you, anyway?" Anna asked in disbelief.

"I'll be nine next month," Sergei answered, looking up with a smile as his hands kept dancing over the console.

"Nine? And you're...doing whatever you're doing?"

He laughed. Gannar smiled and she couldn't help but follow. Steve just turned the chair he was leaning on and sat, looking at the blinking lights in front of him.

"I've locked that keyboard, so don't think about crashing us," Gannar said.

"Crashing? We're underground," Steve said, as the ancient viewscreen on the front wall went white and then pixilated to life.

The spaceport was moving away very quickly. There was a new crater sending smoke up into the air. The city was a speck a moment later, then the whole world was a brown blur and then a brown marble.

"What did you do?"

"About two years worth of work," Sergei answered. "It would have taken me another ten if Gannar hadn't come looking for me."

"Well, I didn't know about you. I came following another lead," Gannar clarified. "Are you out of the gravity well?"

"Don't hover, Gannar. I know how to pilot a capital ship."

"Capital ship?" Anna and Steve said together. They looked at each other, then at Gannar.

"I didn't just salvage the stairs, kids," he smiled. "We rebuilt the ruined ship."

"A fugitive from justice has a functional capital ship," Steve breathed. "Mom is going to flip."

"That's why you want to take them home," Sergei chimed in. His smile lasted a few seconds, replaced by a pouting frown. "Let it go."

"Just like you let things go?" he said. Serg shrugged again. "Genes, Serg."

"Is he...your son?" Anna asked. "Eight would be...that's not possible."

"They are brothers," Sephalos answered. "The both have the Trilouis nose."

Anna looked. Serg was little, so it was hard to see, but the same angle was there and the same odd flat spaces near the eyes. "Rene is your father?"

"His too," Serg smiled.

"I knew that."

"I sometimes have to explain things to slower people," he sighed, spinning his chair to look at them.

"Are you neglecting your flying to gloat?" Gannar asked.

"You're hovering. We're set. I'm waiting for the word from the captain."

"Since when have you listened to me?"

Sergei shrugged. Anna just watched in confusion.

"Mr. Lofkren, engage," Gannar boomed, a smile on his face, pointing at the stars on the viewscreen.

Sergei tapped a series of buttons on an ugly metal box welded to his console. It was a different metal than the rest of the ship and it didn't belong. Anna figured out it was the telephase generator just as the metal started to glow orange. There was a change in the air. Static raced around the ship.

The Academy sat outside the viewscreen. Anna jumped up, her mouth wide open. Steve glared at Gannar, then stood next to his sister, leaning on the back of a chair.

"We traveled that fast…," Anna whispered.

"It's the generator. It's powering this ship," Steve said.

"One of five in existence," Sergei smiled. "And I wired it in."

"Yes, you're bright. Now get a docking tube ready before someone shoots us down."

"You have a generator. You're insubstantial to anything they can shoot at you in defensive mode," Steve added.

"It was figurative, Sephalos. I've made my point and now I want you guys to be safe."

"Where are you going?"

Anna turned, remembering what had been said a moment late. "Wait, one of five?"

"The fleet has three," Steve said at the same time.

"Which question do you want?" Sergei called out, his attention on the screen, where the hollow plastic tube was snaking across the black space near the station.

"I'll handle both. Anna, we are heading someplace the Fleet won't find us. And that's all I'm telling you. For your own protection as much as mine. And Steve, yes. Five. You're on your own to figure that out, but don't ask too loudly or you'll be crewing for me."

"Don't be ridiculous," Steve said, but the way Gannar looked at him, he paused.

"Tube locked. There are about fifteen Fleet Security types in spacesuits starting to crawl the outside of it toward us."

"You two better get moving," Gannar said. He grabbed Anna and gave her a hug, then held out a hand to Steve.

"You're a thief and a traitor. I'm not shaking your hand."

"I can respect that," Gannar said. "Just keep an open mind when you're busy hating me. And remember, five generators."

"I'll take them to the airlock."

"No, they can go on their own, Serg. I have a feeling Steve would grab you and make a run for it."

"He could try!"

Gannar shook his head, sighing. "Down the hall, first left. Move fast because we're cutting the tube loose as soon as we can."

"Or sooner. Some of those guys are climbing fast."

Anna hugged him again, feeling how he was much thinner than before. It wasn't like the muscular hugs when he was her age. Steve just stalked to the door and waited. "Come on, Anna. That kid will space us if we endanger him."

"Yes, I will," Sergei answered, with that same smile. Anna still gave him a little wave on the way out the door. He nodded back at her, raising a little blond eyebrow in surprise.

Chapter 37

The headmaster leaned back, steepling his fingers in front of his pale face. He sighed, leaning forward and flipping through the papers on his desk, then leaned back again. "I have reviewed the reports you both submitted and I have forwarded them to Fleet Command. I have to say, it is a serious breach for you both to have…"

The door slid open, interrupting him. "Excuse me," he started, but the two men that entered weren't the sort that listened. Both were fully armed and wearing not only tactical suits, but the special ones that could be sealed as temporary spacesuits. Fleet Marines. The toughest of the tough.

Elizabeth Cosgrove entered a moment later. She wore her usual skirt suit, in the plain blue color of Fleet dress uniforms. She didn't look nearly as well dressed as usual, Anna thought, because the shoes weren't perfectly shined and her hair wasn't styled into submission. She'd rushed.

"I need to speak to my children," she said, staring at the headmaster.

"I am in the middle of an interview. They will be available soon."

"Shut up. Get out."

He sat up, anger in his eyes. He was showing backbone, which made Steve smile. Whatever she was looking back with, his look lasted only a second. "This is quite improper, even for you Admiral."

"File a report, then. Like you did already, through open channels where everyone could read it."

"I have a duty…"

"Get out," she screamed. He grabbed a folder and moved quickly. When he was out, the Marines nodded and stepped into the hallway. The door closed behind them.

"What did you do?"

"This Sergei engineered the whole thing, on Gannar's…"

"I know, Anna. I read the report. I'm not an idiot. How did you get involved in this? How did you not apprehend him?"

"How could I?" Anna asked.

"How could you, he's your brother, or how could you, he was armed and never let you near him?"

"We did not have an opportunity, mother," Steve added as the two women stared each other down. "I was stunned and Anna had a broken arm. We were unarmed and aboard a ship we had no way to pilot if we seized control."

Elizabeth exhaled, looking at her son with a glare he returned. "No one is going to believe that. It's already circling Command that you're in league with your brother. They are talking about taking me off the Oversight Committee because my family is compromised."

"What can I do?" Steve asked.

"Stay here. Study. Be a good student. Do everything the Fleet asks of you."

Anna looked at her brother. It was very familiar to what she'd heard before. Just very different, too. "Me too?"

Her mother's look was far from happy. "Iris Belmonte won't walk again. Vida Hernandez may never have full use of her left arm. Shannon Lotmiler is dead. These were some of my best people."

"I'm sorry. I didn't…"

"That's right. You didn't do anything. You didn't use your pilot training or combat training. You sat back and waited."

"I'm a kid. They were under attack and tried to protect me. They had orders to keep me safe. I couldn't ignore orders and run into a fight just to fight."

"When have you ever listened to me? I didn't expect you to ignore an attack. You're going to be a terrible officer and there's nothing I can do about that. Just try not to embarrass me. Graduate and disappear into your mediocre job."

"Thanks, mom."

"Don't get smart. You disappoint me. But I can't yank you out of here because now the whole Fleet is watching you and waiting for you to get in touch with that thief."

Steve smiled. Anna wanted to punch him. "I'll do my best, mother," she said.

"And neither of you say anything. To anyone. Ever. Understood?"

They both nodded. She looked at each of them for a couple of seconds, then marched off. The automatic door almost wasn't fast enough, but Anna didn't feel like laughing despite her mom's little stutter step that almost put her nose into the door.

"What just happened?" Anna sighed as the door closed, putting her head in her hands.

"Iron Betty," Steve said. "Just like we always heard the stories."

"I don't know why..."

Steve stood up. "She's right, Anna. A Fleet officer has a dozen duties. You should have stepped up and helped out. With a sufficient force, we may have been able to capture the traitor."

"Sufficient force? They were shooting each other!"

"They were Fleet people. They would have banded together when the true threat was known."

Anna shook her head. "The Fleet isn't perfection in a uniform, Steve. We're all just people doing our jobs."

"That's the bad attitude that prevents you from being a success in the Fleet," Steve yelled back. His raised voice caught her by surprise. If anything, he'd been quiet since they returned. Quiet since he told her about Mayberry.

The door slid open and the headmaster walked in, straightening his uniform and frowning. He slapped his files back on the desk and sat down, staring across at both of them. "I can't imagine there's anything left I can say that will put any fear for your career into you, so let's just move on to discussing demerits and how you'll catch up on missed work..."

ABOUT THE AUTHOR

T.M. Thomas lives and works in western New York.
Check out more at tmthomas.com